T0161514

SOME PHANTOM
NO TIME FLAT

TWO NOVELLAS

Stephen Beachy

VERSE CHORUS PRESS

Published by Verse Chorus Press
PO Box 14806, Portland, Oregon 97293. versechorus.com

Front cover image © Galyna Andrushko/Shutterstock

Book design by Steve Connell/Transgraphic (www.transgraphic.net)

ISBN 978-1-891241-36-9

Library of Congress Control Number: 2012950267

PRAISE FOR *SOME PHANTOM/NO TIME FLAT*

"Henry Miller said that the moment you have an original thought, you cease to be an American. These 'fissures in the architecture of the Dreamtime' are great unAmerican novellas."

—Thorn Kief Hillsbery

"Writing that seems to emerge out of the landscape of the new American West itself . . . Emotional states—loneliness, terror, longing for escape—get blown across these bleak scenes and become entangled, the way the second of the two novellas slips out of the first, like a growth, and turns into something totally unexpected. There's a lot here that's been plain to the eye for a long time. No one's said it so precisely."

—Alvin Lu

"Stephen Beachy has created a disturbing text that reaches from a darkness below our cities' streets, where children, desire, cruelty, and dissociation meet in a shadow land that readers will sadly recognize as contemporary North America. Suspense builds toward surprising, metaphysical conclusions. The work is creepy, desolate, and rich. Do not read before bedtime."

—Stacey Levine

"These two novellas are smart, spooky, and very, very observant."

—K.M. Soehnlein

"The preternaturally talented Stephen Beachy offers stories about alienated, marginal drifters and sexualized criminality without the hackneyed plot twists, pat psychological explanations, or lurid descriptions these subjects usually engender . . . Fans of intelligent noir will be delighted with these gems."

—Alvin Orloff

BY THE SAME AUTHOR

The Whistling Song
Distortion
boneyard

SOME PHANTOM

It's only but a small hole
In my chest
But there blows
A terrible wind
　　　　　—Henri Michaux

1

She'd been dozing in fits, slumped against the bus window, but wakes now into a world of salt flats and sunset. She feels guilty about sleeping through such magnificent landscapes, the way she used to feel when she fell asleep at the movies. Some significant plot development or telling clue may have been irretrievably lost, and she was never the sort of person who could molest other filmgoers for their version of what she'd missed. Nor did she entirely trust them. Later, she decided that some films almost require that you sleep in fits. You wake, and a conscious planetary ocean looms above you. Your dreams mingle with the dream of film. The salt is like foam on the endless earth, a vast crystallized underbelly.

Later, the evening star comes out. Still later, the moon.

The hotel is stone, but the interior is faded. No ID is required. Back in the bus station it was all contorted medieval faces, too close, as if asking questions, making demands, harsh lights and vending machines and unintelligible crackles from the intercom. Now, blown free from the swirl of the station, she rests in the shabbiness she had hoped to find beneath the elegant facade. Safe.

Only her frugality has ever led her into contact with the sordid. The sordid doesn't fascinate her; she wants to soothe it. She sits on the bed, which sags slightly. Watches her reflection in the mirror, unknotting blond hair from the top of her head. *A woman escaping from a horrible crime.* She is exhausted and unmoored in the cosmos. *Nothing ever rests. Then what is death?*

Is she thrilled? She supposes that this must be terror, but it doesn't really suit her. She's too easily distracted. She takes the cash from her purse, and counts it. Having paid the weekly rate for this sad, efficient room, she's still left with a dangerous sum. Shouldn't she be able to find a real place to live in a week, if she wants to? With enough left over for a first month's rent and deposit, plus some. If she needs another week here, things get harder. She doesn't require much in the way of food, but there's bus fare to think about.

She takes two twenties and places the rest of the money under the mattress. Too obvious, but there really isn't anywhere else.

Maybe she won't even stay here. She doesn't have to, her bus ticket will take her on and on, as far as she wants to go. This country is full of cities.

Down the hallway, hopeless red carpet. The desk clerk is reading a newspaper, doesn't even look up as she goes.

The city is immaculate, heavy, abstract. The buildings are monumental, the park lit by yellow globes. Married couples stroll through it arm in arm, as if stepped from the pages of a catalog advertising the blandest styles one could hide in. She is back among the trees, dreaming of life.

Wanders away from the downtown, into residential areas with narrower brick streets between the white homes, which form an immense compound. Girls are perched behind the glass of second story windows, as if placed there for some effect. She's heard that the religious of this city keep their young women locked away from the world until they are married, although she'd guessed that fact was probably exaggerated or somehow inaccurate. She tries to make eye contact, but all of the girls are gazing at the sky. She ties her hair in a translucent blue scarf instead, becoming a mystery.

Men stand idly on the street below, pretending not to watch the girls. Hands in their pockets. She puts on her sunglasses, hurries past. She likes to think of herself as something that rushes past, like the wind.

Emerging onto a major boulevard, with a donut shop and cars gliding past, she reorients herself to the specific dark splotches that are mountains. The sky is a sheet of aluminum foil. The air is so pure, she feels as if she is breathing, really breathing, for the first time in years.

She walks several blocks, finds herself in front of a comic book store, now closed, and a tavern with light and noise spilling out the curtained doorway. This would be what passes for the seedy part of town. The glimpses of garish subterranean worlds on the covers of the comics promise "psychological depth," but she knows from experience that the contents of the thought balloons would disappoint her. The endings would never be terrifying enough. Only the imaginary landscapes would be comforting, alleys of permanent darkness, like the streets she's been wandering, but filtered through an overwrought imagination. In any case, they're all on the other side of the window. She steps into the tavern, for warmth. The men at the bar turn to see, then as apathetically turn away. She hears a high pitched laugh from the darkness at the far end, where a pool table is not being used.

Orders a hot chocolate with peppermint schnapps. A kind of celebration, she decides. Her new life will start tomorrow, and she is still in that transitional zone, where the rules of everyday life are suspended.

Oh, she says then, realizing why there are no other women in this bar and why the men are so indifferent. She feels, again, safe.

That's four dollars, says the bartender and she cringes. She pays, lets it go. Halfway through the drink, exhilaration rises into her face. She turns to the man next to her.

Excuse me, she says. But I'm new in town.

He squints at her as if he can't imagine what she might be driving at.

In fact, I've only just arrived. I plan to stay. I mean, I feel that I've decided that much.

I've seen this one, he interrupts, and gestures to the tv screen overhead.

A blonde woman is laying flowers on a grave.

It doesn't end well, the man says.

A man in a car is watching the blonde woman, from a distance.

For the woman? she says.

For everyone.

You want me to tell you? he says. Or you one of those people like to be surprised?

Surprises are probably overrated, but she certainly wouldn't choose foreknowledge. Anyway, he says, you were saying.

Yes, she says, I was wondering. If there's work here, and if it's a very expensive city to live in. Have you lived here long?

He laughs, as if to himself.

Most people have, he says. I mean people tend to *stay* here more than they *arrive* here, if you know what I mean. But it's a cheap city to live in, if that's your worry. Where you staying?

A hotel near here, she says. The Baker.

She remembers the money wadded up under her mattress and thinks that she shouldn't have named it.

Oh no, he says. You don't want to stay there. You want something nicer than that, I mean the Baker . . . I've spent many nights in the Baker, you know what I'm saying? It's not the sort of place for a sweet young thing like you.

She isn't sure if he's mocking her, she feels neither sweet nor young, but when she catches her reflection in the bar mirror, she sees clearly that she *is* a sweet young thing, relatively. This too is youth, she had discovered over and over again, and feels delighted, expansive.

At least you're not at the Wayne, he says. That's when you know you've really hit bottom, when you find yourself at the Wayne. You can do better than the Baker. Ten dollars more a night you can stay at the Starlight, just two blocks down, but the clientele is more . . . it's a tourist place, you know, retired couples. The ones that travel around in their silver tubes.

She's irritated at the implication that she can't take care of herself, but nods to appease him and, thinking about the money says, Yes, I'll move first thing in the morning.

She sips her warm drink. His romantic phrases probably come from the pages of the graphic novels next door. "Hitting bottom" is what those characters do; they enter worlds where it is always night. The first person you meet in a city is very important, she decides, because they will shape all your perceptions. They are necessarily an omen. She decides to find out more about this man.

Later, back on the street, she feels relieved to be alone again, looks over her shoulder to make sure she's not being followed. She knows

SOME PHANTOM • 11

it's ridiculous; she's only letting her imagination create unwarranted drama in this exotic setting. Exotic? It's so self-consciously *normal* that it's *extreme*. In her room she checks the money, counts it, and moves it into a drawer, between the pages of the telephone book.

She wakes in the middle of the night; it sounds like water is rushing through the stone streets. Is it water or a swarming of rats? Probably just the plumbing. She could leap to the window to see seafoam or rodents glistening in the moonlight. She loves the idea of what the night harbors. The night never frightens her. She drifts back to a world of pursuit and amusements.

In the moment between dreaming and waking, she hears the voice of a shadowy figure who resembles a detective, a curious man with intimate knowledge of her fears—leaving her throughout the next morning with the faint impression that she is being watched.

She breakfasts at a Taco Bell, on cinnamon twists they call *churros* and coffee. In the daylight, it's a different city, a city she never would have chosen. The people had seemed harmless and pathetic, but their day faces are furious masks. How is a sense of mystery created, she wonders. If you understood its construction, you'd be altogether lost. There's probably something pleasurable in that. She picks up a newspaper that somebody discarded, pleased that she's saved thirty-five cents. The newspaper's anxiety masks the riddle of the booth's surface, which is imperturbable. Smooth, shining, cartoonish. She hollows tiny ribbed packets of salt into her palm, licks it up.

On the front page the largest story is that of a boy who arrived in the city on a bus last night, with a note from his mother saying she could no longer care for him. The boy is only twelve and is being embraced by all the tendrils of the city's network of social service agencies. The picture shows a group of concerned "authorities." From clues in the story she determines that this child arrived from the same direction she did, at approximately the same time. She doesn't remember a boy like that on her bus. She was, however, attending more to the landscapes.

She can imagine herself as both the abandoned child and as his tired mother, desperately needing release from the ceaseless demands of other creatures. She wonders if it's possible to be too empathetic. It might get in the way of survival. She tries not to fool herself about her own nature.

Elsewhere, a parasite is suspected of having contaminated the raspberries. At the raspberry festival, aggressive raspberry farmers gorge themselves, smear the berries around their lips.

At the bottom of the front page a headline reads Mysterious Ice Worms Discovered. *Scientists diving by submarine amid the oil fields of the Gulf of Mexico have discovered vast colonies of previously unknown worms burrowing into a great mound of methane-rich ice erupting from the sea floor. The rosy pink worms, barely two inches long and blind, bring new proof that life is tough in the extreme. From scalding hot springs to rocks deep underground, evidence has emerged in recent years that living organisms can flourish almost anywhere on Earth. By implication, the discoveries suggest that life could be possible on many other planets and*

The article is continued in the back of the paper. She flips to the want ads instead, begins circling studio apartments. There are many reasonably priced places, although she hasn't oriented herself enough to know which neighborhoods she would or wouldn't want to live in. They're all carpeted here, how awful.

He had always loved to rip up carpets, to rip up linoleum, to find the wood underneath. It was her job then to sand the wood and stain it and varnish it, to keep it nicely swept. Soft woods like butterscotch, smooth under her bare feet on a sunny morning. Without her, his floors will go bad. He must be pacing them, desperate and enraged. *Unless he is already on her trail.* She turns to the Help Wanted section, circles ads for Residential Counselor or Special Ed Teacher's Aide.

If she had been born here, inside this Taco Bell, what myths would explain where she was, where she had come from, where she was going? Infinite tranquility and evenness of texture.

She makes a few calls from a pay phone. Thirty-five cent calls add up quickly, especially when they lead to nothing.

She eats only a cup of soup and some bread for lunch.

She can't become sluggish and bloated, or she'll be caught in the open. Exposed and devoured.

At dusk, on the streets again, the city changes.

When she imagines her childhood, it's set on a vast wheat plain, under an enormous sky. The land and the sky blur and merge in a haze of summer heat. The little girl lives completely alone in an old farmhouse, wearing sundresses and hair to her waist. She sits under a tree and imagines that in thousands of years she'll be something that doesn't die or even think. By then she won't even be the electrical process of thought itself.

The girl is always alone. Endless summer heat and light and dust. The house is her stomach. She searches for lizards speckled brown and grey, motionless and easily mistaken for sticks. Others which change colors, moss green, brown as roots. They can transform their skins without a thought, cover their tracks. Do they themselves forget where they've been and what they've been doing? She is fascinated by the various mechanisms of survival. Secreting unpleasant odors. Poisonous underbellies, coloring similar to dangerous organisms.

2

The school's windows are fogged, as if sunlight is too harsh for these delicate children, who can only be raised by moonlight or overhead fluorescents. The school smells like some combination of antiquated disinfectants, powders, and casseroles. It's a children's center attached to an elementary school. The interview is brief. The principal is clearly impressed by her résumé, but worried that she's one of those idealistic young white people who'll get tired of coming into this neighborhood to work. Oh no, she says, that isn't me.

The school I used to work at wasn't in what people thought of as a nice part of town, she says. But the people were very nice.

Back there, you could walk all the way from the center of town to the ocean, through eucalyptus trees in the park.

She'll have to get her TB test and her fingerprints and police clearance, but in the meantime she can start working. She won't be paid, however, until all her paperwork is done.

How long will that take? she asks.

The principal, a woman with bad posture, shrugs. It's the District, she says. You never know with the District. A couple of weeks if there aren't any problems.

The shift is 8:30 to 1:00 with a Special Ed class of three- to five-year-olds. She'll meet the teacher and the kids when she reports to work tomorrow morning.

She has to take two buses back to the downtown. The trip takes almost an hour. She would like to pass the horrible afternoon hours riding buses at random, seeing the people and the landscapes at a distance. She picks up a discarded fragment of newspaper. The city is congratulating itself on all it has done for the unfortunate boy who was left by his mother. The outpouring of aid is offered as evidence of the city's benevolent nature. There is a photograph, but you can't see the face of the boy, who is surrounded by caring people in sweaters. She wonders how they could be wearing sweaters in this heat but remembers that the nights get cold.

Moonlight fills the hotel room. She sits in front of the mirror, brushing her hair. He used to run his fingers through it, but sometimes he couldn't resist grabbing her by the hair, hurting her just a little bit. He accused her of liking it, as if that alone was proof of her infidelity: if she liked him to treat her roughly, wouldn't she like it from any stranger? And then one day she found herself in a different life. Now, in this strange place, what happened seems like a story she's told herself, a story of origins in which she "hit bottom." It's a story that serves only to explain her present circumstances, which would otherwise be a random configuration of meaningless elements: moonlight, hairbrush, strange noises in the plumbing.

Because she can't sleep, she walks the streets. The girls in their windows are dreaming of the savanna. They are racing through the tall grasses in the pink light of dusk. The men on the street below are like fat antelope. The girls enjoy their hunger too much to feed. The moon is fat. The moon is finally waning.

She comes across an adult bookstore and guesses she must be near the "seedy part of town." She turns corners at random and finds herself in front of the comic book store, which is brightly lit, with the doors wide open. A teenage boy is unloading boxes from a van, through the store, and into a mysterious back room. Music is playing, spacey and Arabic sounding, with synthesizers and moaning women. Stepping into the store is like walking onto another planet.

The boy ignores her, and there is nobody else around.

This one seems to have a plot similar to a movie she once saw. It's become quite common: somebody is dead, but they don't yet know it. She wonders if the violence she is fleeing was worse than she realized.

She could be fleeing her own murder. She heard once that ghosts were composed of the memories they couldn't let go, which was why they tended to haunt familiar places. Ghosts don't travel long distances, except in that movie. She can't think of any particular memories she cares that much for. Therefore, she is a human being.

On the cover of another book she sees a prim woman wandering down a dark street in a generic-looking city of night, replete with neon signs, overturned garbage cans, and eyes in the shadows. It's a ridiculous, corny image, but somehow compelling. She flips through. The actual story line seems more complex than the cover would indicate, and the illustrations are simply yet intricately drawn. The woman on the cover has a teenage son, only glimpsed. He is peripheral, always in his room, until he disappears and the mother's life is thrown into turmoil. The story becomes a mystery.

She read comics as a child, of a biblical nature. The men had overly large muscles and wore revealing outfits. With the most rudimentary lines and dots, a "handsome" face could be created. She wonders how much the mystery costs; it is slim, and so maybe inexpensive. Maybe tomorrow she'll forego lunch.

Hello? she calls into the back room.

Hello? Is there anybody there?

The walls of the classroom are covered with colorful alphabets, drawings of houses and suns, art projects made out of macaroni and beans glued to construction paper. The room is actually two rooms that open onto each other, but the far room remains empty, lights out.

The teacher, Becky, is barely older than she is. The other teacher's aide is Ben. He's younger, with curly reddish hair and a goatee, grey eyes. A big guy, and tanned. He could easily be a figure from a biblical comic, a warrior with an open, trustworthy face, or an evil king who might or might not repent. He might be a character who saves women and children, or he might be a fallen angel. The buses with the kids are waiting outside.

There are eleven now, but they're expecting two more. Thirteen is the legal limit in this school district.

Somebody in that bar had changed the channel; she would never find out how the movie ended. She touched that man's arm. I often felt like I was a gay man trapped inside a woman's body, she told him.

You need a more original thought, he said. Maybe you're a woman trapped inside the body of a woman.

He had waved his hand at the new movie on the tv. Any second-rate actor decides they need an Oscar, he said, all they got to do is play a retard.

He pronounced it French, *ritard*. She liked the sound of it, it sounded like status. It put her in mind of a movie she saw once, it was either French or about the French. Insane people were made out to be revolutionary. She told the man in the bar about it.

Back when I was a kid we used to say *mental*, he said. Now that doesn't sound so bad, does it? *Mental*.

The day begins with Circle. At Circle, the children are introduced to the concept of time. Days of the week, months and date and holidays and weather. Is it cloudy today? asks Becky. Cloudy, repeats a tiny boy, giving her his complete attention. Are there clouds outside, she coaxes, or is the sun shining? Sun shining, says the boy, triumphant. Meanwhile, Circle is falling apart. Children wander off. A small boy with beautiful long red hair, who she initially mistook for a girl, hits the boy next to him. She hopes for instruction of some sort from Becky. Keep an eye on Jessica, says Ben.

Jessica is the tiniest of the children, just turned three and small for her age. Jessica takes her hand and leads her to a number chart on the wall, grabs her finger and touches it to the chart.

She wants you to point to them and say their names, says Ben.

She runs her fingers through Jessica's long black hair.

Forty-three, she says. Forty-four. Forty-five.

The girl is deliriously happy. What the girl really wants is love, she thinks, but when she stops naming the numbers, Jessica shrieks like she's been slapped. Toys are flying, other children are screaming. Ben is running every which way, putting bad children in chairs. At Circle, Becky continues bravely, with four attentive children, singing *The wheels on the bus go round and round, round and round, round and round*.

After Circle comes Snack and then Playtime and Recess. At Recess, she can finally catch her breath. The children are dispersed among the Regular Ed kids, and there are plenty of teachers supervising. The school is on a hill and the playground floats above the city, with the downtown and the mountains visible in the distance and enormous puffs of cloud almost directly horizontal. In the other direction, she can see a shimmering line—the plain of salt on the outskirts.

After Recess, there is more Playtime, which drags on forever, and then Lunch. After Lunch, things really get wild. The sand table explodes, children hit, throw blocks, put things in their mouths that aren't food. Crayons fall to the floor and scatter. The children aren't supposed to cross over to the other side of the room, to bother those toys, or the fish, or the rabbit that sleeps there. It is madness. Jessica tries to drag her back to the numbers, but she ignores her and tries to break up a fight between Noel, the red haired boy, and a boy named Samson. Jessica falls to the floor, screaming and hitting her head. Just ignore her, says Ben, unless she really seems to be hurting herself. At this point Becky asks her to take her fifteen-minute break.

The teacher's lounge is a tiny windowless room with a bulletin board, four chairs and a small table with a microwave and a coffeepot on top. There's a Coke machine. In red and blue marker on a sheet of pale construction paper tacked to the wall it says

Together
Everyone
Achieves
More

Sections of newspaper are scattered across the table. The headlines are of a city betrayed. It seems the twelve-year-old boy abandoned by his mother has turned out to be a young woman in her twenties. She disguised herself in an attempt to scam food and money from the innocent. She can't find the information about how they finally caught on to the deception. The picture of this woman has been cut out of this particular newspaper, but the caption is still there. The story makes her feel sick to her stomach. Not the woman's actions, but the townspeople's. Not town, she reminds herself. City. She closes her eyes. When she hears the door open, she wishes she were invisible. A large woman smiles at her, but doesn't say anything, and sits down.

Another woman comes in and starts talking to the first as she digs plastic containers of lunch from a paper bag and spreads them across the table. They are discussing coffee. I was off coffee and onto tea, says the lunch eater, and then I married a Lebanese man.

They drink a lot of coffee? says the first.

Do they drink a lot of coffee? They drink it strong, I'll tell you that. She closes her eyes again.

You can leave me, he said to her once. Just don't ever go off somewhere without telling me where you are. I'd go crazy, I really would.

He said that because he knew vanishing would only ever be her only recourse. He would never really go crazy without a witness; without a specific witness. The very real threat of insanity existed only as long as she was there.

She picks up another fragment of newspaper. Glancing through it, the themes that emerge are of crime and punishment: graffiti, gangs, prison bonds, minor political scandals. *Fueled by teen boredom and the influence of charismatic ex-cons linked to prison gangs, big city–style "gangsta" culture is steadily catching on among kids throughout the county according to police and family counselors.*

She rises as nonexistently as possible, smiles meagerly at the women and goes back to class. There is only a half hour until the buses come. Jessica, who seems to have been screaming the whole time she was on break, stops, lies quietly for a minute, comes and takes her hand and leads her to the bookshelf, picks a musical alphabet book off the shelf. Becky suggests to Jessica that she might enjoy the art project at the big table. They are dipping pinecones in peanut butter and bird seed, to make bird feeders. Noel, the red-haired boy, eats both the peanut butter and the bird seed. Jessica becomes involved in a life-or-death struggle to place her pinecone exactly *so* on the table, but it keeps rolling out of her control. This process threatens to develop into a screaming fit as her frustration combines with Ben's misguided efforts to help her. Clearly he doesn't grasp the exact nature of what she is trying to do or its import in balancing her cosmos correctly. Noel gets bored, kicks Samson. He claims to be a Power Ranger. Ben sits him in a chair for Time Out.

It's time to clean up, clean up, clean up . . . , the teacher sings. The children ignore her. Miraculously, somehow, the children assemble their backpacks and jackets and get swooped up by several tiny yellow buses. That's it, says Becky. You can go. Have a good weekend, says Ben.

She follows Becky back into the classroom, collects her jacket and her purse. Becky seems exhausted. Do you have any questions? she asks.

Questions, she says.

She looks around the classroom.

You've worked with children before? Becky asks.

Yes, didn't the principal tell you?

Mrs. Couchman doesn't tell me anything, Becky says. I cause too many problems. Mrs. Couchman just wanted Special Ed here to look like she's doing something, but she doesn't really want to deal with us.

Becky laughs.

Across the room, the rabbit makes a scratching noise. She tries to think of something to say.

Jessica, she says.

Yes, says Becky. Have you worked with autistic kids before? She exhibits a lot of autistic behaviors, but she's making some progress. We try to discourage the numbers and the alphabet stuff, she's just stimming. Wait until you meet her mother.

Becky rolls her eyes.

Addicted to heroin when she was born.

Uh-huh.

Approaching footsteps echo in the hallway and move past. The room itself is unnaturally still and dusty in the absence of the children.

She sits with Becky at the table, now smeared with dried peanut butter. The kids' files are laid out before them, Becky preparing herself for an Individual Education Plan the next morning. Becky tells her how she was lured here from her home state back east under false pretenses. They told her she wouldn't have to take any more classes, that her credential was good here, but it was all lies. She was trained to work with older, SH kids, that's what they promised her, she doesn't ever want to work with SED kids again, but they're getting two more kids, both of them SED.

SED, she says.

Severely Emotionally Disturbed, says Becky. You ever work with SED kids?

Yes, she says, but I'm not sure if it was official.

She laughs.

I mean I'm not positive what the label was, she says.

She thinks that maybe she shouldn't have made light of diagnostic process. You never know what silly beliefs people subscribe to.

In this district, says Becky, kids get SED as a last resort. You know, the parents and the teachers and everybody wants them in a Special Ed class, and they have some behavior problems, so they're SED.

This statement reassures her that they are at least not diametrically opposed in their views of children, of children's souls.

It's not whether or not they're really SED, it's what's the best place-ment, Becky says. This is definitely not it.

Becky gestures as if to indicate the classroom or the whole school or the vast inappropriate universe itself.

They promised me no SED, she says again.

It's all a disaster. The principal ignores Becky completely. The pre-vious aide was a teacher of Russian who'd lost her real job because of budget cuts. She hated small children, wouldn't let them touch her. One day she just stopped coming.

They told me I wouldn't have to do any IEPs, Becky says. And here I have to do IEPs for every single kid. I have an IEP for Lupita tomor-row morning.

Mind if I take a look? she asks.

She leafs through the kids' folders, case histories, diagnoses.

Who's this? she asks. Dimario?

New boy, says Becky. Supposed to start next week.

Pages and pages of psychiatric tests and family history. How a four-year-old could amass such a volume of literature . . . Dimario's mother was addicted to cocaine when he was born. He displays atten-tion span problems and aggressive tendencies. He's lived at times with his mother and older stepbrothers, whom the report notes as "negative influences who model inappropriate behaviors" and his grandmother, whom the report seems to approve of. He is plagued by nightmares and often talks about monsters and eyeballs. Dimario is quoted as saying

"I'm gonna stomp on your eyeballs" several times to social workers and therapists. He has many fears. Dimario is a bright, handsome boy, the report says.

And we can't let them go on the other side of the room, Becky is saying, because Mr. Wagner'll flip if anything is out of place. What's the point of an open classroom?

A bright, handsome boy. Seems like a code for something, she's not sure what. She returns Dimario's folder to the stack.

The after-school kids will be here in a half hour, Becky says. They'll leave their art projects sitting around and of course our kids destroy them. I get blamed. What kind of a situation is this? I don't have any time to plan in this room. You've seen the teacher's lounge.

She feels like she's supposed to say something. The point of an open classroom, she thinks, is to teach the kids that the most important walls are invisible.

I talk to the District, Becky says, and the District says to talk to Children's Centers and Children's Centers says to talk to Special Ed and I talk to Special Ed and they can't do anything because they have no jurisdiction over the school as a whole. They can't make the principal do anything.

She flinches, as if Becky is going to slap her. Mad face, she thinks. Mad face, sad face, silly face.

I guess we have to make the best of a bad situation, she says.

Right, says Becky.

There's an awkward silence.

Okay, she says. Then I'll see you on Monday.

Her bus carries her through suburban streets and past strip malls and auto dealerships, nearer the center of town. Attached to the Sheriff's Department is a small room where she waits to be fingerprinted by a man who is busy filing papers. After about ten minutes, he glances at the clock and sighs. Okay, Ma'am, he says. He rolls her fingers through black ink and then rolls them onto cards. Just relax them, he says. Let me do all the work. See that? Smudged. That one's no good at all.

He takes out a fresh card, rolls them again and scrutinizes his work.

Pretty soon we won't need the ink, he tells her.

Oh? she says. She has no idea what he's getting at. He pats his computer like it's a faithful dog.

All be in here, he says. All be zeros and ones.

The screen is completely blank except for a blinking horizontal line in the upper corner. As soon as she leaves, she thinks he'll type in her name.

That's ten dollars, he says.

Oh, she says. I didn't know I had to pay.

He just waits.

Will the District reimburse me? she asks.

He doesn't respond. He doesn't seem to be processing anything more until he gets paid. She digs two crumpled fives out of her bag.

As she leaves, she pauses outside the door, and listens. She can hear him in there, aggressively clicking on his keyboard.

She waits for her bus at a transit center in the middle of nowhere. It may be the "middle of nowhere" that creates the feeling she's being watched. It could be him. Or in this city, it could easily be a sex offender. That phrase reduces her anxiety, it's so absurd. Sex offenders are not supposed to be as entertaining as serial killers. As a victim, her outfits would be skimpier. She sees a bus that says SALT PALACE in front. Does this go out to the salt plains? she asks the driver. She had been afraid he'd look at her like she was stupid or insane, but he simply nods, distracted.

After passing through several interchangeable neighborhoods that look like they were built in the sixties and seventies, the bus passes through an older, slightly industrial part of town, with brick buildings and railroad tracks. The bus stops at an overgrown sign and a stone bench and the driver gets off, shuffles around the corner of a rundown brick building. It is silent but for the sound of boys playing soccer on a slanting field up the hill. The sunlight is everywhere. She doesn't belong here, but it is also as if everything were placed perfectly for her benefit. She thinks that she was supposed to feel united with Becky in unspoken outrage that Jessica's mother was addicted to heroin when she was pregnant. She forgives the teacher for trying to bond, trying to share a moral context. The afternoon here is enormous and hushed. The boys have fallen on each other in a heap and she can't tell if she hears cries of pain from the bottom. The heap is lasting too long. Is that bare flesh or tan slacks? She wonders if one on the bottom of the pile or one on the top would be described as a bright, handsome boy. The driver returns with a styrofoam cup, and the bus wheezes on. She looks back until the boys are lost from sight. Through development communities outside of town and business parks. The bus passes these forlorn neighborhoods and other lonelier ones. Beyond all this there's snow in those mountains, rabbits eternally nervous. Wouldn't it be easier just to be eaten now, get it over with? An owl startles the daylight. Out here past the neighborhoods, it's like blood in the snow. She is so sleepy, like she's been working all day.

She's the only one to climb down from the bus at the end of the line. The salt stretches on, occasionally interrupted by upcroppings of black rock. The driver sits reading his newspaper, doesn't look up as she leaves. The Salt Palace is a rundown art deco-style building. It looks closed. She walks in the opposite direction, across the salt.

The light is everywhere now, blazing and white. She carefully removes a thin black kerchief from her purse and wraps it around her hair. To protect her hair from the salt, she tells herself, but smiles, knowing that it is really for a visual effect which there is nobody to see. Her footsteps crunch crunch crunch. The salt is in the wind. Behind her, the bus starts again and wheezes back toward the city.

She's that woman from the Bible, transformed. The night before, she had entertained an angel. The angel was terrible to behold, a shapeshifting mass of faces and mutant animals and body parts with a dazzling pink light around the edges. The inside and the outside were painfully confused. It was beating on the outside. The angel hid its grotesque infinity inside the body of a charming boy. Men did battle in the streets for him. The wind at dusk.

The earth is flat and endless. She hopes that when that cop looks for her information, he'll find a perfect emptiness like this.

Nothing stirs. She arrives at a small cluster of rocks. Insects flit about her face, thin and juiceless. She kicks over a rock. Something is moving there, pink and translucent. Some sort of larva or worm.

No, not just one, a whole cluster of intercoiled pink worms. She uses a stick to dig the salt away from the edge of the group, but can't get underneath them. They seem infinite, a complex system of roots leading into the heart of the earth. As if this mass of blind and naked bodies, just underneath the thin crust of salt, composes the earth's very substance. She tries to extract one of the worms but the bodies are so intertwined that she only succeeds in tearing off the head. The head continues to squirm between her forefinger and thumb. She drops it into the salt, where it contracts and then stops.

In the distance, a car pulls up in front of the Salt Palace, and a group of people make their way inside. From the way they move, she judges them to be old. The merciless light reflecting off their puckered skin.

The sunset here is a fascination. The earth gives up its heat quickly. The old people never come out.

3

The woman is going through her son's email for clues. The language is truncated or oblique and she can barely understand it. Dense little bundles of words sprawl across panel after panel. The mother is discovering that the boy she thought she knew is a complete stranger. He has written to somebody: *i'm functioning like myself in school again. and sometimes i feel happy (which is a GREAT change from before). feeling more out of it again, but i think that's due to lack of sleep and other stresses—hallucinagenic sortsa things, my imagination is intense. when i woke up this morning my friend told me bout her brother that, while sleeping, walked downstairs, asked his granny for a burger, ate it, and went back upstairs. and i said that we're all probably sleep walking to some extent. u know?*

The comic book store is empty. She flips ahead a few pages. The mother is still trapped at the computer. She flips further. The mother is traveling now, searching for her son, breaking down. The mother's descent into madness isn't as interesting to her as the mystery of the absent boy. Who is he? What has been done to him? What has he done to himself to create himself? She enjoys being manipulated into caring. She is mesmerized by an absence that is a larger presence than the presence ever was.

She skims through other graphic novels, hoping to find one in which crimes are committed by alter personalities. She loves stories in which virtuous people wake up next to corpses, or surrounded by clues as to their own guilt.

Although it is only Saturday night, she has purchased the Sunday Want Ads and spread them across the carpet of the hotel room. The tap drips in her little sink.

Plumbing is a mystery. The pipes of this structure should be dried out, cracked and corroded and layered with salt. The thought of water is too disturbing, the moist living things the dampness engenders. Anemones and silverfish. A sea cucumber eviscerates itself. It hurls its innards at predators to repulse those who would consume it.

She unfolds a translucent map of the city. Letters of the newspaper underneath bleed through to create a map for a different city, abstract and esoteric. She circles apartments with a pale orange marker. The language in the newspaper is so coded, she can't figure out what it all means. Every floor is carpeted, and they even brag about it.

Generally there would be an area near the university with decent bagels and coffee shops, older houses with wood floors, reasonable rents. She must be careful. It must be easy to find someone, once they have an apartment. A blinking dot in this vast computerized surveillance network. He wouldn't know how to utilize those resources, but he could hire somebody who would.

For him, everyone was a mirror sending back a warped reflection. Her lover. He lived in a fishbowl. His body ballooned grotesquely as he observed. Some days it was puny, some days it was fat.

She opens her windows all the way and lets the cold air blow through her. She could walk through the streets of the city again, return to that bar, where that man would still be sitting. He was always there, in that bar, she decided, every night of his life, and if he didn't show up, the other regulars would know something catastrophic had happened. Habits make you easy prey. Perhaps freedom must consist of a conscious resistance to habit.

That man said that evil was a collective process. Was that it? Why had they talked about evil? He had sold coupon books over the telephone as a younger man.

We misrepresented, he said, without actually lying. I became learned in the art of salesmanship, bullying and cajoling. I convinced people that if they used only five of these hundreds of coupons they would make their money back. Once the book was sold, a delivery person was quickly dispatched to collect, before they could change their minds. Or before they could articulate an adequate response to our bullying sales pitch without losing more face. They did not possess the vocabulary of self-righteous indignation, and we took advantage of this fact. I possessed it, for I was raised in the church. Not buying our worthless little collection of 50-percent-off dinner coupons at painfully inadequate restaurants was an injustice against common sense and communality, family values, and togetherness. Did they not eat out with their families? Go bowling? What sort of people would not benefit?

She can hear music in the distance and she shivers. She is alone. She was alone before, once, all the time, and created herself as a minimal landscape. She gave that then to him, as a gift. She had hoped he would fill that landscape with intricate structures and music and glass and so it began. A shared language that nobody else could understand. But then the shapes were only halfway formed. He was unable to translate the music of his soul. It wasn't hidden from her, but she was not enough.

Beauty is a certification of health, her lover told her. It's all a matter of biology.

Oh no, she said. Certainly not.

He had some ideas about where the world was heading, and these ideas got mixed up with his own life and behavior. He became so unhappy. His unhappiness grew, like the structures of some misconceived plumbing spreading into the darkness beneath them. And then it mutated into something harder to recognize.

I'm from here, the man in the bar had said, and it is a sad comment on my personality that I remain here still. I could blame *them*. They have little tricks that make it harder to leave. Like those children raised by wolves. The dialect they speak here, it gets inside you and it feels like home. But it's my own fault. I have no courage, no drive. I've chosen a life of opposition to the familiar over the fear of finding a place more compatible to my nature.

They send you out when you are young, he said. To proselytize.

He laughed at himself.

So I gained my experience of the world through meetings with strangers I was trying to manipulate and trick into believing something

I didn't understand myself. It was all scripted and intense. I was terrorized by the loneliness of such contact in such strange landscapes, and I have never gotten over it.

What are you running away from? he asked.

Why do you say that?

People don't just come here, he said. Unless they join the church or they're a ski bum. Or a con artist. Church people don't wander into bars like this one, and your skin's too pale and smooth to be a skier.

You're quite the detective, she said. Pleased that he would take such interest, still vague enough to remain unthreatening.

A detective, he said. You mean I'm snooping, a voyeur. You mean I'm someone who puts my own desires onto other people and calls them a crime.

She said, I guess you like to figure people out.

Maybe I should say *who*, he said. *Who* are you running away from. Not the police.

No, she said, not the police. Nothing so glamorous.

Then it can't be a stalker exactly.

No, she said, not exactly.

What had been gradually filling the time between them was a regime of exercises and internal debates about exercise. Should he spend his time doing squats or swimming and running? She decided that his physical motion in the world was his way of feeling, his art. He wanted to move like a man.

Something is falling from the sky. Flowers of iridescent plastic drift earthward. It could be parachutists are floating into the city, soft and silent as cat burglars. An invasion or a practice invasion? She doesn't know if there's really a difference.

He had always required a witness, but less and less was her reluctant encouragement what he asked for. Perhaps he barely notices now that she is gone. But that's ridiculous. *Whatever you do you can't ever just disappear.*

But he had made anything else impossible.

The last parachutists drift down out of sight. She waits for something to happen. Some sort of local festival maybe, or else they are just here among us now, indistinguishable. They won't need to fire a single shot to take over. A gradual transition of values. She leaves the window open, the cold breeze coming in gusts.

Sunday morning she is up early, coffee and *churros*, making her telephone calls. Answering machines don't do her any good. She is scandalized by the coins she wastes trying to reach landlords who are sleeping late or gone to church. Finally she gets through, makes an appointment to visit a studio apartment just blocks from downtown. She leaves herself time to walk there, get to know more of the city.

Knowing her mother will be at church, she splurges on the long distance call. Leaves a vague, cheery message, assuring her mother that she's fine, that she'll call back once she gets settled in, although she doesn't reveal where it is she's settling in at. Her mother is the first one he'd try. Perhaps he has already taken over Mother's home, tied her up and gagged her, and is even now playing the message over and over again. Listening for clues, as her mother looks on in bewilderment and terror. *Bewilderment and terror* is such a familiar combination of words. Is that how the world really works? She has to admit she's not sure what her mother would be feeling at all.

Standing on a corner, she notices a woman at the bus stop clutching an infant. Compared to her bright, unnaturally cheerful Sunday morning surroundings, the woman seems disenchanted, desperate, and wise. She looks familiar. Her first thought is that she's the woman from the news, the woman who took advantage of the city. But that's ridiculous, they didn't even show that woman's picture in the paper. She remembers that that's not exactly true. The woman has short hair as the con artist must have had, to pass herself off as a boy. The woman stares right at her with a crafty, conspiratorial look, as if about to do some crime that might involve her. She thinks that the woman is about to toss her baby in front of the bus. She wonders if people do this all the time, never get caught. Killing a baby is the easiest thing to do. They are so fragile. Oops, they say, I dropped my baby. Unfeeling people can often cry convincingly. She should offer some vague kindness to this woman, take the baby into her own arms. It isn't as bad as all of that, she'd say, and perhaps the woman would really cry. The woman seems to give up on the bus, walks on, her baby intact.

The apartment is lovely, wood floors, and a nice tree out the window. The landlord is a garrulous retired man.

If you have bad credit, he says, tell me now. Just be honest, I can work with you, but there's no point trying to hide it. I can find out anything. I can find out what you had for breakfast this morning.

She shakes her head. Her credit is fine. He talks about how well he gets to know his tenants, the bonds he has formed with tenants in the past. He talks about his world travels, the Eastern rim, in a way that implies extensive knowledge of the prostitutes there. He hands her an application, tells her he requires a $25 nonrefundable deposit for the credit check.

I'll take it with me and get it back to you, she says.

It's better if you fill it out now, he says.

No, it's better this way, she says.

She hurries down the street, around the corner. She crumples up the application, tosses it in the next trashcan she comes to. Hurries on, as if she has somewhere to go.

New student today, Becky says, gritting her teeth.

The morning is misty, almost rainy. The buses are lined up like toys. Jessica climbs down, happy, with her pacifier in her mouth, followed by Lupita, Noel, and then Dimario. He's wearing a puffy, oversized jacket, as is the style, and brand-name tennis shoes. His head is shaved, with a little tuft left at the nape of his neck in a way that seems stylish, not just convenient for grooming. She is startled by the accuracy of his file; he's a handsome boy. He stops and looks around.

I'm at Dr. Charles Drew, he says.

Hi, Dimario, says Becky. I'm Becky, your teacher. And this is Ben, your other teacher and . . .

That sing-songy exuberant tone that drives her crazy. It's so condescending. She thinks Dimario must see right through it, have nothing but contempt for it.

Ben is calmly staring at the boy. She thinks that it's the same way her lover looked at her when they first met. That look came to no good, not for anyone.

Dimario's face is so alert, he's taking everything in.

Come on, says Becky. We'll show you your new classroom and you can meet all the other kids.

Did you hear him? she whispers. *I'm at Dr. Charles Drew*. He doesn't belong in this class.

Shaking her head.

Good job coming in and sitting at your spot, you get a sticker. Noel, sit on your bottom and I'll give you a sticker.

Noel, says Dimario, sit on your ass.

Becky gives him a forced smile.

Here at Charles Drew, we say *bottom*, she says.

They do Weather, Calendar, Singing, Shapes.

A box is a square, says Becky. Some books are squares, and look! Our floor has squares in it. What else is a square?

A tv show is a square, says Dimario.

Very good! says Becky. She moves on to Triangles, then does the closing song.

Good job at Circle, Dimario. Everyone who did a good job at Circle gets a cracker.

Becky asks her to hand out Triscuits.

They look like they made of grass, says Dimario. Are they made of grass?

No, she says, looking at the box. Actually, they're made out of wheat.

Yuck, he says.

Mmmm, she says, just a little bit ironically. Wheat's delicious.

They look like they made out of bones, he says.

You know, she says, that's true. They do look like that, but they aren't, not really. They're made out of wheat. It's delicious and it has a lot of vitamins.

He looks her over.

What happened to your eye? he asks.

Oh, she says, I hurt myself.

But that was a long time ago, she adds. It's better now.

He looks skeptical, as if he knows she's not being completely honest with him. As if he's a boy who can handle the truth.

After Circle he wants to see the fish. He keeps running over to the other side of the room.

It's okay, says Becky. Just for today. Just make sure he doesn't get into any of the toys.

Ben takes his hand, walks with him to the aquarium.

Becky touches her arm.

He speaks in complete sentences, she whispers. *Appropriate* sentences! You see what I'm saying? Never mind the behavioral stuff. Never mind his influence on *them*. He doesn't have any *peers* here.

Now the other children want to see the fish. It is like a contagion, this desire, moving through the classroom in visible waves. Becky sighs.

One at a time, says Becky. You have to just go over one at a time.

It's a small studio near the center of town with wood floors and chicken-wire tile in the bathroom. The windows look onto a communal backyard with a fountain and a persimmon tree. The woman who's showing it is from an agency, young and officious. Her name is Debbie.

It's a good neighborhood, says Debbie. Very convenient.

Children play in lawns across the street, boys and a girl. They seem unnaturally loud. You're it, says the biggest boy.

Convenient, she says.

Shopping's just around the corner, says Debbie.

Debbie's smile is hard and cheery, her hair in a ponytail, but when she turns away she looks annoyed. The other children run off, leaving the youngest boy alone.

Lots of families, says Debbie.

You have kids?

Debbie gives a little shudder.

Kids these days, she says. They give me the creeps.

She isn't sure if she heard her correctly. The boy seems to be pinching himself, and counting.

When would you want to move in? Debbie asks.

As soon as possible, she says. The room I'm in is paid through tomorrow, so Wednesday would be perfect.

Fine, Debbie says. I can meet you here Wednesday with the keys and the lease, say eleven?

I work until one, she says. How about two?

Debbie checks her schedule on some electronic contraption.

Two thirty?
Two thirty would be fine.

The afternoons are the worst, out in the world. It's a horrible place.
There are drainage ditches of the sort that dead bodies are found in.
There are fragments of overheard conversations that refer to unimagined desires. If she was a ghost, but didn't realize it, it would be her
own life she was reading about in the newspapers of the world. In that
movie she saw about this state, some woman kept encountering the
faces of the dead. She was an unbeliever, a church organist and was
already herself drowned, but didn't know it. She was located halfway
between two worlds. Reality flickered in and out. She only played
the organ with feeling when she was possessed by the collectivity of
the damned. The film was starkly beautiful, a bleak grey miasma. It
was like a dreamed version of this state without the searing light and
monument, a few degrees off reality.

Like her, the church organist had worn her hair tied sometimes in
scarves.

In the seedy part of town, she finds a movie theater that shows both
adult and older films. This afternoon it offers that movie she'd seen
part of in the bar.

It's cool and dark inside. The plot hinges on a ghost story of sorts.
It isn't that the ghost is real, but that the woman who will kill herself
seems to believe it is real. After the suicide she reappears, either her or
her ghost or her double, but with a different color of hair. The detective tries to make her into the original image he'd been tricked into
loving.

Before it ends, she gets up and goes back out into the darkening
city. The sky is the color of eggplant, but liquid, explosive. Purple
nitroglycerine. There's supposed to be a comet visible but she can't
find it, can't locate any of the relevant constellations. She feels exiled
in the distant corner of an empty outer space. Where the flow of solar
wind finally ends and there's nothing but void.

At school, the sun is so bright, so glaring outside. Inside, the fluorescent lights are cold and detached. The adults barely speak to each

other. It is like this: they speak to the children when they want to com-
municate. Maybe Ben will read you that story, Becky says to Lupita.
It creates a strange world of autistic gestures and children's songs,
mimicry and single-word sentences that make up her social universe.
She tells herself it suits her, but it leaves her feeling sometimes a little
bit unreal.

It is primarily the wind on the playground. The air is cold and sunny
and the clouds so near they are like bulbous brains. The wind is moving their thoughts along and the sun and click of footsteps and jacket
zippers. The light is changing.

At recess Dimario asks her if she's scared of birds.

Sometimes, she says, if they're very big.

I'm not scared of birds, he says. I scare birds.

When I run at them, he says, they fly away. They think I'm a killer.

He runs off. She waits, leaning against the brick wall, hoping he'll
return. But she doesn't get to talk to him again until Playtime inside.
The children are playing in the sand, in the House, with the blocks. He
seems initially overwhelmed by all the options but quickly bored.

You wanna watch a movie? he asks.

He has three little plastic people and some toy cars.

Yes, she says. What's it called?

It's called Killer Dream.

He starts crashing the people into each other and the cars.

And this guy says why you wearin your hat backward, you look
like a punk and he says why you say that and he says KPOW and oh
why'd you do that the police is gonna come and put you in jail.

His monologue occasionally turns into musical accompaniment.
The fogged window has a stripe of clear glass at the top through which
she can see the flag flapping in the breeze outside. Always seems like
the loneliest thing. The last remnant of some alien world that is still
somehow going on. Clouds sailing past in the breeze. It's like some
poor organ beating in the sun.

Did you like that movie? asks Dimario.

Yes.

Did you like that part where he got killed?

No, she says, not that part.

Did you like that part where he socked him?

No.

Did you like that part where he fell down?

No.

Did you like that part where they were playing?

Yes, she says. That was a good part.

Oh, he says. That was the part you liked.

Somewhere in the school, she can hear a telephone ringing. But there aren't any phones here, she thinks. But then she remembers that of course there are phones. It's only her hotel room that doesn't have one.

4

She wakes, sure she's heard a rooster. Steps to the window to see if the sun's really rising. The quiet and chill and first outline of the mountains. She'll almost miss this room. Having a "home" will make her feel lonely.

She must be pregnant. A knot of blind albino snakes in her belly. A hysterical pregnancy, she decides. It's begun to rain, and the city is transparent in the wet air. She gathers her things together. She'll go directly from work to her new place.

Helping the children off with their slickers, Ben is always tickling Dimario, touching him. He takes the boys into the bathroom. She hears Dimario laughing and laughing. The rain will keep them inside all day. At Circle Dimario insists on sitting on Ben's lap. She's disappointed with herself for feeling jealous over the affections of a four-year-old. They sing *Five little monkeys jumping on the bed* . . . They sing about peanut butter and jelly, they sing about the wheels on the bus. Dimario straddles Ben's knee, squirms around a little excessively.

Circle disintegrates and the children are off. Dimario is still bouncing up and down on the knee.

Where do you want to go, Dimario? she asks. Blocks or House?

Blocks! he says, leaping up, but just stands for a moment watching other children run here and there. House, he says. Come on.

She follows him to the House, where Lupita and Robert are already serving a plastic carrot and pouring imaginary juice into cups.

Man, says Dimario. My mommy drinks beer.

Grown-ups drink beer sometimes, she says, but we drink juice at school.

Does your mommy drink beer? asks Dimario.

Lupita never says any words except *Barney* and *Mickey Mouse* and with a lot of coaxing, *please.* Mommy drinks beer, says Robert, who doesn't understand questions, but repeats everything.

My mommy drinks juice, she says.

Man, Dimario says, itching his belly, I'm gettin *more* mosquito bites.

He leaves the House and goes to the rug, dumps out a box of Konnectos, little plastic cubes of many colors you can stick together in various ways. She follows. He begins connecting them very seriously.

What are you making? she asks.

It's dangerous, he says. Put this electrocutie here.

Oh, she says. It's electrical.

Be careful, he says. Put this electrocutie here or it'll burn you.

How's this? she asks.

That's good, he says. Put these here or it could kill you.

Noel approaches, flushed and intense. Dimario tells him to stay away, because it's dangerous, and if he doesn't Dimario will stomp on his eyeballs.

You're playing so nice, she says to Dimario. You don't need to talk that way.

Sorry, he says. Here, put this electrocutie like this.

After Lunch she sits with several kids cutting pictures out of magazines and pasting them onto construction paper. Jessica likes to paste and Robert likes to cut, although he's not very successful. Dimario isn't interested, plays with Ben and the Play-Doh. Feeling a little bit rejected, she focuses on Jessica. Jessica is a fearless child. There is something admirable about the way she lives in her own private world of mysterious signs and meanings. She wonders if she identifies too much with such a brave and lonely task. Despite her occasional tantrums, she seems like a happy child. Jessica takes her hand, leads her to the books. She cannot reach the musical alphabet book so points at it, tugging on her sleeve. She picks up both the book and the girl, brushing her lips against Jessica's ear.

At Rest Time Dimario comes to her, lays his head carefully in her lap.

She doesn't have any chairs yet, or even a table. She piles up a blanket, comforter, a couple of pillows to make a bed. Hopefully, she'll get paid soon. She counts out the days. *Monday, Tuesday,* she starts singing to herself, *Wednesday, Thursday, Friday. Saturday and Sunday: the days of the week!*

These songs will drive her crazy if she lets them inside her head. She arranges her few things around the new place. A music box, a candle holder, clothes, a small mirror, toiletry items. It's so sparse. The only furniture is a chest of drawers that was left behind and a built-in bookshelf.

She didn't have to pay so much deposit, so she's ahead of the game. She has over five hundred dollars left and her check shouldn't be more than four weeks away. The thought that it could take longer than that makes her a little bit angry, and then a little bit worried.

She checks the mail, because she's always needed to check her mail every day. Among anonymous coupon books and a mailer with missing children on it, she's surprised to find a plain envelope with her name typed on the outside. No return address, no postmark, it must be from the rental agency. One of the missing children looks like Dimario. No, on closer examination he's not nearly as striking. She sits on the porch, opens the envelope. It's a beautiful textured ivory card, but all it says, spelled out in letters cut from magazines, is WELCOME HOME. How strange. Is it the agency trying to be homey? Somebody from work? Nobody from work knows her new address and it isn't postmarked. She tries to suppress her growing terror with calm, ordered thinking. Rental agencies don't write notes in letters cut from magazines, kidnappers do. The neighborhood is quiet in the drizzle, nobody in sight.

He's found me, she whispers. Hearing her own voice in the hushed neighborhood frightens her. He's somewhere close by.

Don't be silly, she says aloud, to calm herself.

Surely it's the rental agency. They tried to make a bright, colorful welcoming message, dumbly oblivious to the more sinister overtones. That's just how people are.

She puts the message away in a drawer. She'll ask the rental people about it next time she sees them, she decides, actually hoping she'll have forgotten it by then, but knowing she won't.

The drawings of the boy's room are claustrophobic. The level of personal detail is embarrassing, but what it reveals is vague; it is unclear what his interest is in the musicians and fictional characters and celebrities and wild animals on his wall. To somebody else the boy has written: *i just realized that i said that I hope to hear from you but my email didn't really contain anything so substantial for you to respond to! so I tried to unsend it but you had already received it. So i re-read it and realized that it's a WHOLE lot of ME's and i's and so I just want to apologize. I didn't mean to give you a synopsis of the role sexuality plays in my life . . . although I guess I was in a way, because your last email had a lot to say on personal sexual experience . . .*

She is the only one in the comic book store again; it feels as if she is the only one on earth, reading a magic book that will tell her who she is. The message is continued in the next panel, which shows the mother's wrist clicking the mouse in a way that suggests physical pain. *But what I wanted to do was further a discussion about sexuality based on, of course, personal relevance. wutever. So again, my bad. you know a lot about my own sexuality now (probably more than you wanted to) and please don't feel obligated to respond to anything i've told you. If you even are interested in this correspondence at all anymore then i'd still be thrilled to have this personal access into your mind! I have to write a paper on a Sylvia Plath poem now. the poem "Mirror." If you've read it, what do you think of it?*

The idea that she is a kind and virtuous person strikes her as a made-up story just as arbitrary as the things this mother believed about her son, which were several years out-of-date. I'm so cold, somebody said to her once. But he wasn't cold, he was acting the part, she knew that. He kept saying it over and over: I'm so cold. He'd been through bad times, many people had died. What was his name? If you believed something about yourself, it might become true. *I'm a kind woman with a good heart; I care.*

You're a little bit distant, that man in the bar had said to her finally. He said, I bet you don't believe in much save the drama of love. You're cursed with it.

I've discovered that those who cultivate friendships are happier in the long run, he said, than those who cultivate love.

Knowing that doesn't stop me either, he added.

She had turned to him, flushed with intimacy. I remember that movie, she said, about that girl with sixteen personalities. I always wanted to be like her. To have all those possibilities.

Feeling as if she'd confided something more revealing than an actual history. He rolled his eyes.

Of course, he said. We all wanted to be that girl.

She thinks that can't be true, not in the same way. She had pretended her own self was fractured, made maps of names for the different pieces. In the years since that movie came out, the process of fragmenting had become a kind of cult. True believers would argue that she wasn't pretending, she was only pretending to pretend, as a way to cover up the real fragmentation of her personality. She found true believers exhausting, but the stories themselves she adored.

Rainy days continue. Unable to go outside to play, the kids grow more violent and destructive. They show them *The Lion King*, *Pocahontas*, Barney videos, to keep them out of trouble. How quickly they get bored, run wild. Dimario is absent, and she feels depressed. She tries to spend as much one-on-one time with Jessica as possible. The alphabet begins to bore her and by the end of the day she recognizes a horrible anger growing inside her, toward the children, the teacher, the walls of the school. She squeezes their hands a little too tight. The rain continues and the next day, Ben is out too. She thinks that Ben and Dimario are together and feels jealous. During Circle, the phone rings. Noel and Robert are fighting, Jessica is wandering toward the other room, Gabriel is staring out the window as if planning to make a break. Would you read them a story? the teacher asks as she dashes to the phone.

She picks out a book about cheetahs. Except for their children, she reads, female cheetahs remain alone. The male offspring usually leave the mother as a group and may remain together for life. Cheetahs feed on animals like gazelles and impalas. The chase lasts only about twenty seconds and it exhausts them.

She wishes that Dimario were here for this. She thinks he'd appreciate it. She thinks that Dimario is somehow beautiful as a cheetah is, but in an essentially different way. She thinks he's some kind of genius. When the teacher tells her that Dimario will be out all week, he has chicken pox, she's relieved that he isn't with Ben.

They do the macaroni necklaces, they do the paper-plate turtles and the paper-plate bear faces with cotton balls. Ben is back and then gone again. He's good with the kids, says Becky, I just wish he wasn't out so often. We never get a sub.

The kids like him, she says.

It's good to have a male, Becky says. Especially for the boys, they need that. They're so short on males.

Everyone says that, she says.

But the world is full of men, she thinks. And look at what's happened.

Supposedly the District is getting a thousand new computers, Becky is saying now. Supposedly in a couple years we'll all be plugged into the internet.

The sun comes out at recess. A teacher's aide with the Regular Ed kids comes and stands next to her as she leans against the wall. She's an older woman with strong opinions about recent events in the news. Which class are you with? she asks.

Room 3, she says. Special Ed.

Oh, the woman says, scanning the playground, that's good. They need good people for that.

Have you met the elementary teachers in Special Ed? the woman asks. She shakes her head no. Some of those kids, she says, you can't even tell by looking at them.

She peers at the woman for a moment as if confused, then decides she has to get away. She looks around for a child in need of attention. Noel, she calls, no kicking! Chases him down, sits him on the bench.

Becky pads over in her sensible shoes.

Since Ben's out, Becky says, could you take your break now?

She hates going into the teacher's lounge with those other people, so sits in the classroom, on a tiny chair, her head resting on the cool table. The table is smooth, but smeared with dried Play-Doh. What peace. Their voices out there, so distant, murmur of clouds and winds and moons sailing among a black and star-riddled sky. They exhaust her, these children. She has so little energy to begin with.

Becky has left some education magazine out with a picture on the cover of a boy seated in front of a computer. That must be why she was rambling on about the internet. An adult has his hand on the boy's shoulder, nurturing him, and the boy looks back, smiling. Because he can have some kind of a future, she guesses, now that he's acquired these skills. A computer screen is a square too, she thinks. She misses Dimario.

The next day Ben's back. After school he is waiting at her bus stop.

You don't usually take this bus, she says.

I'm going to visit my friend, he says. He's sick.

The other people waiting for the bus are old and tired, except for one young woman who should be in school. She looks old and tired too.

I hope it isn't serious, she says.

He shrugs. He moves his hands as if to begin a gesture that would accompany what he was going to say, but stops short.

Nice park, isn't it? he says.

Here, just down the hill from the school is a small green area, with trees and a playground. Swings, silvery slide, and fake horses that bo-ing up and down.

We bring the kids here sometimes, he says.

She tries to think of something just as innocuous to say. They have never spoken about personal matters, through a tacit understanding that during work hours none of them is a complete or even real human being. They are modulated voices of love and authority, masks hiding the fundamental horror of the world, there only to respond to the needs of the children in appropriate ways. This has suited her perfectly, because she isn't ready to think about her old life. It is enough now simply to be living a different one. She knows that someday she will have to cry, not just once, but over and over again.

The bus arrives and she boards quickly, so that she can sit first and leave it to him whether to sit next to her, across from her, or completely away. He sits next to her and she is relieved, for it seems the least awkward arrangement.

Becky said she thinks Shedrick and Demian can go to regular kindergarten next year, she says.

That's great, he says. Demian's only problem is that he gets so shy. God knows what's going on in that boy's life.

Becky said another teacher saw him wandering down on Third Street by himself.

He nods.

They pass several identical neighborhoods. She tells herself that she ended up here because it's the loneliest place in the world. He takes a toothpick from his pocket and unwraps it.

Are you from here? she asks.

Me? He laughs. Oh no, I'm not from here. I'm from out there.

He waves his hand backward, dismissively.

America, he says. It's all pretty much the same isn't it?

She pictures a vast landscape of houses and mountains and freeways and antennae and glittering junk. She saw a desert once, to the windward side of a city. The trash blew and blew.

Why'd you come here? she asks.

Good question, he says. I guess I just ended up here. I had to leave the city I'm from. Got too small.

He picks at his teeth.

There's something here I like, he says. A certain innocence that's appealing.

He laughs.

Not that the people here are as dumb as they pretend to be.

She looks slightly shocked.

Oh, come on. You know what I'm talking about.

She laughs, relieved that he's been able to observe something in her interactions with the children that is contrary to the nature of this place.

I guess you're right, she says. It just sounds so . . . harsh or something. But no, I know just what you're talking about.

She shrugs.

I've been living on the coast, she says.

She feels like naming the city would reveal too much, lead to certain assumptions.

It's a little bit different, she says. The edges are different, I think.

That's true, he says.

She thinks he said it as if he's been around. They ride for a moment in silence. She thinks that they've reached the limits of their intimacy for now.

You make it with just the one job? he asks.

For now, she says. How about you?

I have another job, he says.

He turns away, as if watching something out the window.

Noel's a trip, he says, isn't he?

Noel? she says. What do you mean?

I mean the way all his moves are straight off the television.

Right, she says. Little Mr. Power Ranger.

Something's not connecting in there, Ben says. I don't think cause and effect really registers for him. So punishment doesn't do anything. He's not a mean kid, he just doesn't get it.

She shakes her head at the sadness of it.

Michael on the other hand, he says, he looks for abuse. He's always on the ground. He provokes the other kids, he wants to get strong-armed.

You think so? she says.

By not immediately agreeing with Ben she feels like she's accusing him of something.

You're probably right, she says.

Plenty of kids willing to do that, she says, to change the subject.

She feels like they both want to talk about Dimario. She holds back.

A few, he says. But Dimario, you know, he talks the talk, but he's no bully. Not really.

She's not surprised that he's perceptive about the boy.

No, she says. He's a sweetie.

He's very bright, says Ben.

A bright, handsome boy, she thinks, and wonders if he read the folder too. She's twisting the strap of her purse back and forth through her fingers.

You're stimming, he says.

She looks down at herself and laughs.

We all do, he says. Tap a pencil, run math through your head. Repeat phrases from the tv.

As if a person was or could become a magnetic pattern or a frequency. As if a person wasn't a mystery so much as a knot of wounded matter.

Here's my stop, he says.

Oh, she says. Okay, see you tomorrow.

Two blocks later, she realizes he's left his umbrella behind. She hangs onto it, thinking she'll take it to school tomorrow. She likes Ben, he's a little bit odd. But there's something underneath, a little bit scary. That word's too strong. *Mysterious* is less judgmental. He "had to" leave the city he's from. Why's that? Nobody comes here without a reason. Skiers, converts, and con artists the man in the bar had said.

What if it's raining in the morning? He'll need his umbrella. She could drop it off at his house. It might be out of the way, but what else is going on? She realizes she's actually looking for an excuse to see where he lives.

At her transfer point she finds a phone, gets his address from Information. She goes into a mall and finds a bookstore. She doesn't want to actually pay for a map, but feels guilty opening it up in the middle of the store. She laughs at the petty nature of her crime, quickly locates his street. It isn't that far from where she's at.

I was in the neighborhood anyway, she'll say. It'll seem ridiculous, he'll know she has ulterior motives. Which are, what exactly? He wasn't even going home yet, she realizes. Unless his "sick friend" is just a code for something else.

She decides to have a look around the mall. She'll need a few things for the new place, at least a few dishes, so she can cook.

The food court. Glass, punctured, pasty, creamy. She's not sure sometimes if she really likes people much. Their actions. Malls make her feel weird inside. The chill of the air-conditioning. The people are all wearing clothes just the same. Seaweed-like tattoos on the forearm of that one. Fissures in the architecture of the Dreamtime. When she escapes into the parking lot she's purchased only a cheap tinny pot, one plastic bowl. She decided against the silverware; she'll use plastic stuff from the taco place or the school. The pink lights, parking lot, and snow on the mountains. Feels a little bit light-headed, vision on her left side bright with tiny lights as if she's going to faint. She's forgotten the umbrella, hurries back inside. Guesses she needs to eat. The umbrella is still where she left it, on the counter. She buys a bagel from the Food Court, hurries out. It doesn't taste like a bagel at all.

Off the bus into a hushed suburban neighborhood like REM sleep. Sprinklers are running, a hedge trimmer whining somewhere, the overenthusiastic sound of daytime tv, but nobody anywhere in sight. A child's bike in a front lawn and one of those little plastic "pools." The sun beats down on all of this, the sun is so near in this city, and now there aren't any clouds for protection.

He was wrong about every place being the same. This city is different from any she's ever been in. The mountains with their snow and blood. It's like living in the brain of a nasty sleeping animal.

She wonders why more horror movies don't take place in broad daylight. Broad daylight is the most frightening thing. The monster or stalker or alien could step out from behind that hedge a half block away into the middle of the street and stare her down. Or from behind the slick, plasticky sheen of the parked cars. Parked cars glinting in the sun like knives from empty windows. Horror movies operate on the principle that direct confrontation is less frightening than what remains hidden in the dark.

In the daytime, long shots would emphasize the space around people, their vulnerability. Close shots would make the audience worry about what they couldn't see. Medium shots would suggest what might come creeping out from the background. Such direct sunlight makes her queasy. This landscape itself is horror.

She walks past the hedge.

His address is half of a modest duplex. The yard is less kept than surrounding yards, with dandelions and brown patches. She pauses on the porch. Some dim music is playing inside; the screen door is all that separates her from the front room. The smell of marijuana smoke. He used to smoke it, she didn't like it. It made her overly analytical, self-conscious, and paranoid. She would wake the next day with too much food in her belly.

She ought to just leave, this whole thing is ridiculous.

What if he was watching from inside, saw her come up to the house and then turn around without ringing the bell? This is so stupid. They're all adults.

She knocks on the screen door, a little too loud.

Maybe he's in the shower or something. She knocks again, lightly. No answer.

Just as she's turning back down the steps, somebody peeks out of the curtains and calls after her.

You looking for Ben?

Her heart is racing as if she's been caught committing a crime. The screen door opens, a face pops out. It's a boy, about fourteen.

Come on in, he says. He should be back in a minute.

She hesitates.

Oh, she says, really, I just wanted to drop something off for him. His umbrella, he left it on the bus, I have his umbrella.

Well come on in, he says.

He vanishes back into the house. She feels terribly compromised now, but she can't just leave. She opens the screen door tentatively, steps in. It seems so dark inside, and the smell of pot is heavy. The boy isn't here.

Hello? she says.

The sound of a refrigerator door opening from the next room, the tinkling of ice. She sits down on an old sofa covered with a quilt. The boy comes out of the kitchen, hands her a glass of Coke. He's wearing baggy shorts and a white tank T-shirt, plops down in the recliner across from her.

You a friend of Ben? he asks.

I work with him, she says.

She doesn't want to say "at the school" because she's not sure how much this boy knows about Ben. But that's ridiculous.

Are you . . . a friend? she asks.

Sure, he says. We hang out.

His eyes are red. He doesn't look directly at her when he speaks, although he doesn't seem at all shy. She's afraid Ben'll come home while she's here. Her excuse to visit seems flimsy.

There's a bright bluish white light coming from under the closet door. She decides not to ask about it, but finds her eyes continually returning there.

I'm Carlos, the boy says.

I'm kind of high, he adds.

He flips on the television, remotes from channel to channel. She looks around the apartment for clues. Bookshelf on the other side of the room, can't make out any titles, stereo, lots of records, personal computer, cheap old furniture, horrible carpet. The computer is running, with a screensaver of some muscular superheroes in tights. On the coffee table there's a box of reclosable sandwich bags, some weird plastic bottles of colored liquid, unlabeled video cassettes, newspaper sections, a bowl of peanuts, a bowl of condoms.

Man, Carlos says finally, television sucks, and he turns it off. He picks up a bottle of skin moistener, squirts white goo into his palm and starts smearing it on his arms.

I like the way this stuff smells, he says.

It's nice, she agrees, although she actually thinks it's horrible.

You ever see anyone hotwire a car? he asks.

No, she says. Not really. I mean somebody showed me what you do once, but it was his own car. I don't remember which wires it was.

Well I could show you, he says.

He picks a condom out of the bowl, tears it open, tosses the wrapper on the floor. Other condom wrappers are scattered here and there. He blows the rubber up like a balloon, ties the end off, bats it between his hands distractedly.

I should go, she says. I'll just leave the umbrella here. Really, that's all I came for.

She stands, and the shift in perspective makes her feel both powerful and adrift.

Oh, he says. He seems disappointed.

Let me show you something, he says.

He digs around the seat cushions of the sofa, pulls out a pair of handcuffs, keeps looking.

Just a second, he says. They must be in the bedroom.

He goes out through the kitchen. She searches for something benign to be looking at when he returns. She picks up a sketchbook full of geometrical lines, intricate maze-like patterns that suggest landscapes or death. It reveals Ben as obsessive and controlling. It's too personal, she puts it down. A superhero gyrates across the computer screen until she absently touches the mouse. The art disappears. Complicated lists of body parts, sexual acts, and the names of celebrities fill the screen. She turns away, just as Carlos comes back in with a second pair of handcuffs.

He leans back on the couch, crosses his legs and cuffs his ankles together, then twists his hands behind his back.

Go ahead, he says. Cuff me.

She does what he asks.

Tighter, he says. I like it when they're tight.

Now go out on the porch for a minute, he says. Count to a hundred. No, better make it two hundred. Wait. Just a hundred is okay.

On the porch she practices the smile she'll make if Ben comes. Bemused, accepting, game. He was flattering her earlier, she decides, when he said she was different than the people of this city. He wanted to make her an ally. She's forgotten to count, starts quickly, to make up time, then slows down. She wants Carlos to succeed.

When she reenters he's sitting up in the reclining chair, completely free.

Pretty good, huh? he says.

She nods.

You still wanna leave? he says. I'll come with you. You ever see the park?

Which park?

I'll show you, he says. Hold on, I wanna check my email.

He starts clicking at the computer.

You have email? he asks.

I used to, she says. She imagines the blank space in the web of electricity where her name was erased. She watches him select and delete, tries to figure out what the jumbled letters of his screen name might mean.

Do you meet people on the internet? she asks.

There aren't any *people* on the internet, he says.

Although she doesn't understand it, she completely agrees. Okay, he says. Let's go.

He leaves the computer on, but locks up behind them. Once she's out of Ben's place, she feels comfortable with Carlos. He wants someone to be both maternal and nonjudgmental, she thinks. She isn't sure what she's basing this on. The park is only two blocks away, but to find this nebulous mask of foliage in the middle of the wasteland of identical little houses is almost a shock.

It kind of sucks, he says now about the park.

I like it, she says.

They sit on a stone bench, he lights a cigarette.

I brought my homework, he says.

Can I see what you're working on?

We have to make up our own continent, he says, with eighteen geographical features and two cities. You wanna see it?

I'd love to, she says.

Mine's called Gunland, he says, carefully taking his paper out of the notebook and laying it over their laps. I just have to finish these mountains with the colored pencils and these little islands here, these are bullets.

She scans the terrain. The main continent is shaped like a pistol. Smith and Wesson mountains, AK-47 City, Murderville, Blood River, Shotgun Plateau.

That's interesting, she says. Do you like guns a lot?

Guns are tight, he says.

Guns are cool, he says, but my teacher hates it. She can't say anything cuz I'm the best artist in class. This is the best continent in class, it's gonna be, when I finish with the mountains.

He scrutinizes his work.

In our class, she says, where me and Ben work, we don't let the kids play with toy guns.

That sucks, he says.

They turn everything into a gun, she says. Blocks and LEGOs and big foam letters of the alphabet.

Carlos reminds her of a boy from high school who sat next to her in Chemistry. He was in her homeroom too, but theirs was the sort of relationship that was only acknowledged in Chemistry. She was a good student, but not prudish. She would cheat on tests and drink beer on weekends, smoke pot sometimes. She followed instructions to the labs but never understood the larger principles. She got an A in the class while remaining mystified by everything but the Periodic Table of the Elements, which made perfect sense. He would play with the equipment like toys. Then he would borrow some other girl's lab and they would copy the results. He was also tracked in the more academic classes, but had formulated a completely different attitude toward school. If she got out of class, it was approved. It was under the auspices of selling ads for the yearbook that she was out of her third period journalism class, walking through the empty hallway as if she had somewhere to go. Nobody questioned her. She was at her locker when he showed up. He just stood grinning at her. What period is it? he asked, finally. It was a revelation of sorts. That one could not only skip class, but not even know what period it was. You should be in third, she said. Mr. Parker, he said, and giggled. She laughed too; his drone about U.S. History was absurd.

The nature of their relationship clarified. He enjoyed having someone tell him, with affection and concern, where he should be and what he should be doing, and they both enjoyed the fact that he wasn't doing it.

Do you have a girlfriend? she asks.

No, Carlos says quickly. Love's bullshit. I don't mess with that shit no more.

What, did you have a bad experience?

He shrugs.

I don't wanna love anyone, he says. It's better that way, if people love you, but you don't love anyone. As soon as you love somebody, then you got something to lose. And you can't really live if you've got something to lose. You can't be really free.

That's a pretty lonely philosophy, she says.

He shrugs.

Some things that can hurt you can feel good, too, she says.

I feel sorry for the people who love you, she says, if you'll never love them back.

He looks away from her, makes a muscle, squeezes his own bicep.

That's just what my friend says. They say that some things that hurt feel good too. My friend says that I can take a lot.

He's misunderstood me, she thinks. He wants to tell her things, all kinds of things.

The wind blows through silvery treetops. Constellations of leaves like sculptured shells, like her own hysterical pregnancy. Her haunted womb. She wonders how mothers love their sons, as they send them off to war, and then she wonders why that image has come to her just now.

Does somebody love you? she asks.

He looks thoughtful.

That's different, he says. They don't expect me to love them.

He looks a little bit hurt, as if she's accusing him of something.

They don't want me to, he says. They said so.

She remembers the elusive giant squid. Its brain is huge and the oceans are deep. Men haven't captured a live one yet. The process of "understanding" dreams is either necessary to avoid catastrophes, or where human history veered terribly off course.

They all must do it. Her lover had been almost bragging when he told her about the things his neighbor had paid him to do when he was a kid. That man's hunger had seemed like evidence to him toward proving something that all of her assurances would not. You look great, she'd tell him, trying not to sound bored, your chest looks bigger every day.

Then one day they'd been quarreling. She can't even remember what it was about, it was so minor.

Then I'm going out, she said.

Don't you wanna make love?

No, she said.

He hit her. He knocked over the plants, then hit her again.

It's so easy for you, he said. Always so ready to just leave. To just throw all this away.

He ripped his clothes off to stand naked and shaking with rage in front of her.

You never do anything to show you need me, to show you need this. You never listen to a thing I say.

Just sit down then, she pleaded. Just sit then and talk to me.

But he didn't sit down, and she didn't really listen; she was planning her escape.

It had ceased to be her life, to be the sort of life she could imagine herself a part of. Her mind was filled with slogans she'd heard about "domestic violence"; they didn't illuminate or accurately describe her experience, but separated her dreams from her life. She suspected the new life, the one she now found herself in, had always been there running along beside the old one. Her dreams had previously been the exaggerations and fears of an unfolding that was correct and true. But old memories resurfaced, incidents from her childhood that had seemed of no importance now reemerging as defining or undefeated monsters. It wasn't that she'd ever forgotten them, she just never attached them much to who she thought she was. There was a boy once. He'd been hoping to frighten and humiliate her, but she wasn't afraid. She rather wanted to touch it. Another boy was watching. Here, she said, you touch mine. She undid his pants and his bare ass was showing. He came right away. The other boy was silent. The first boy shoved her onto the ground and called her names, then stormed away. Taking flight had seemed like a way to step away from these memories and reclaim the childhood she'd thought she had, of fantastic journeys and open skies.

Don't you get lonely? she asks Carlos.

He sneers.

You gotta be right in yourself, he says. That's all.

Do you live around here? she asks.

He nods.

I'll get out though, he says.

I'm not gonna get into any of that gang shit, he says. My friend said he thinks I could be a model, to make some money. He knows all about how to model and stuff.

Ben? she says. Does Ben say that?

He looks away from her so she can't see his face.

My friend said he thought I could be an artist, he says.

I think he's right, she says.

Is your family in the church? she asks.

He looks at her like she's stupid.

We're *Mexican*, he says.

She runs her fingers over the smooth stone of the bench. Thinks about robots and distance and glass.

We're Guadalupistas, he says, but he's smiling like it's a joke. She waits in silence, staring at the rustling leaves.

I see the girls your age all the time, she says. The ones in the church. Trapped behind glass.

They escape sometimes, he says. There's a girl gang, they live in the tunnels under the city. I know some of them. I met them at the mall.

He's a gullible boy, she decides. The sort of boy who'll believe whatever lie some girl tells him. On the other hand, she escaped. Why couldn't they? She tries to remember if she saw any girls at the mall who were unsupervised and unnaturally pale.

I didn't know there were tunnels, she says.

This city sucks, he says.

He snatches a piece of paper from his folder, crumples it up and throws it toward the hollow mesh garbage can. It bounces off the rim and rolls into a patch of overgrown clover.

But I'll get out, he repeats.

You're very talented, she says. You're an excellent artist.

What do you think of this? she asks, taking the graphic novel from her purse. He scrutinizes the pictures. Too much stuff, he says. It's like you never see her face, just her legs or her hair.

He doesn't care about the plot, but likes the shading, and seems intrigued by the odd angles; he expresses his interest as disapproval. She hadn't realized that there was such an emphasis on body parts, juxtaposed in nonsensical ways. What had interested her was the missing boy. Once he was found and revealed as "beside the point," she'd lost interest. It's kind of perverted, Carlos says. She can't tell from how he says it if that's praise or critique.

He hands it back. There's this computer game at school, he says, and I can build the best cities of anyone. I got hella stadiums. I put my prison on an island so I got my own Alcatraz. The main thing is you gotta get rid of all your trees and mountains very first thing, they just get in the way.

That doesn't sound so nice, she says.

It's just a game, he says.

You sound like Ben, he says. Ben has all kinds of ideas about the future.

About your future, she says.

But for a moment it's as if she's no longer talking to anyone but herself.

I got a whole row of libraries and museums, he says.

I'd like to see your city sometime, she says.

There's no curfew in my city, he says.

He digs his hands into his pockets. An elderly woman enters the park, with some horrible animal on a leash.

Do you have a curfew? she asks.

He looks at her like she's from another planet.

Of course, he says. The whole city does, ever since that boy killed those people. It's just some bullshit. We stay out all night, all they do is take you home if they catch you. My mom doesn't care. It's just that I have to be home by a certain time, you know, if I'm coming home. But a lot of times I just *don't*.

She begins to speak, but then waits, as the elderly woman and her dog draw closer. The dog sniffs at the trash can, leaves scent, and they move past.

Do you stay over at your friends' houses sometimes? she asks.

The most cynical look crosses his face, and then it's just blank. He knows exactly what she's asking.

My good friends, he says.

Daring her to further define the terms. She almost says, Maybe we'll be good friends someday, but it sounds too needy and like it could be misinterpreted in a sexual way.

Young people need their sleep, she says.

He seems deeply and sincerely bored for the first time. He lights a cigarette.

I sleep, he says.

He offers her the pack, and she takes a cigarette. It's been years since she smoked, but that's one less to ruin *his* lungs.

My mom says I'm sexually active, he says.

This statement just hangs there. He grins at the smoke puffs.

As long as you use a condom, she says.

This conversation has to end soon. Realizing this, she's terrified that he'll end it, she can't bear the rejection, but then reminds herself that she's the less vulnerable one.

As if reading her mind, he says, I guess I should get going.

Oh, okay, she says. It is getting late, isn't it?

She thinks of asking him not to tell Ben that she came by but decides it's more important not to build an atmosphere of secrets and distrust. She stands. He looks suddenly so young again, and sweet. He doesn't have anywhere to go, she thinks. His face hardens.

Okay, see you around, he says.

Sure, she says. I really like your artwork. I do hope I'll see you again.

He's not really looking at her, shuffling his feet.

I work at the school with Ben you know, she says.

Okay, he says.

Take care, she says.

He ambles off in the direction they came from. Her bus stop would be that way too, but she goes a different way, to avoid any awkwardness. She stubs out the cigarette, stashes the butt in her purse.

The cigarette has made her feel sick. On the bus she decides he was sending her a message. That thing with the handcuffs.

A desolation in the landscape, the sun lower but still bright in her stomach. She can't do anything for that kid. Can she? They both understand, Carlos and Ben. They understand that it just doesn't matter. Whether you obey the law or break it, whether you get caught or you don't. She is choked with grief. There's a police car parked at the Burger King. The police are a joke. They're enforcing chatter around a hollow center. But the hollowness is bleeding out into all the surfaces.

She gasps for air. She's always known that it doesn't matter, but he never understood that. If you love the right way, the wrong way, or not at all. Love will never penetrate to the core, for the core is empty.

It doesn't matter. It is heartbreaking, and exhilarating. But right now it is only heartbreaking.

By the time she finishes a sandwich downtown, the sky is darkening. The purity of the air, a richness that had nauseated her in the sunshine, now calms her and fills her. Her silly little bout of despair cost her dearly; she's wasted money on an overpriced sandwich she could have fixed herself for pennies at home. She remembers that note in her mailbox and feels glad she's out in the city instead. She walks around the monumental structures. There's an enormous gleaming white building illuminated by spotlights. It holds the family records of just about everybody in the world, at least the white ones. Those that *belonged to the church.* Whom the church owned. It seems to be open like a diner, 24 hours a day. It's absolutely free. The guard in the glass cage is reading his newspaper as she floats past, doesn't even look up.

She glides up and down elevators through long hallways full of file-cases, metal bureaus, computer screens. She wouldn't want to find anything out. She is here just to feel it: the weight of all that information on the earth, as it tries to seep in.

Conversations are going on across centuries, but all we can do is listen and speak to the future. She is not interested. The empty structure of words, as if humans were permanently biblical, is the opposite of the pink trembling light. Out there it's all wind and light and wind.

Surrounded by all this heredity and misinformation a phrase comes to her: *the firstborn of the dead.* City light streams through high tiny windows at the ends of the corridors, inaccessible windows, so that seekers aren't distracted by the living.

She breezes back out into the streets.

A sliver of moon. One of the men draws close to her, keeping his hands in his pockets. She thinks that he is masturbating. She thinks of the horrible things that are going on in the world. They don't matter, they delight her. If she turned to face him, his face would melt or be monstrous. A predator has to be smarter than its prey; their brains are always more complex. She herself might creep through the dark, looking through windows. Carlos and Ben up in that house. She never saw the bedroom, but can picture it. Curtains always drawn, messy, stained carpet. She thinks about Ben and Dimario together in the same way.

5

Wanna see my chicken pops? Dimario asks as he climbs off the bus.

She gives him a quick hug.

It's good to have you back, she says. We missed you.

I hear you met Carlos, Ben says.

She smiles at him as sweetly and sincerely as possible without over-doing it.

Oh, she says. Yes, I was taking your umbrella back. You left it on the bus. I was in the neighborhood.

That was sweet of you, he says.

He seems like a very sweet boy, she says, then realizes that repeat-ing the word "sweet" sounds weird.

He likes you, Ben says.

He seems like a good kid, she says.

At Circle Dimario insists on sitting on Ben's lap. He's into the knee. She's afraid Becky will notice the way he's squirming. Ben's vibrat-ing his leg ever so slightly. She's relieved when they do the Shake Your Wiggles Out song and Dimario leaps up, gets crazy. When the confusion is over, he's standing next to her. She holds out her arms, welcomes him into her lap.

At recess Ben plays ball with some older SED kids. A second grade girl named Precious starts screeching and attacking the other children, and Ben grabs her from behind, drags her toward the building.

Get away from me! she screams. You smell like drugs.

He says something to the girl that she can't hear.

She walks toward them to help.

You smoke, Precious says. You do. You're keeping secrets. You stink like drugs.

She wants to shut this little girl up. Shove a sock in her mouth, or put her in a room somewhere. But she isn't the one being accused, she's not the guilty one. The girl's teacher shows up on the scene, takes Precious off Ben's hands.

He stinks like drugs, she says again.

You can't smell that out here, her teacher says.

Ben is smirking. She wants to grab that hateful little girl by the throat and choke the life out of her. Oh no, she tells herself, I don't want to do that.

She says that about everyone, the girl's teacher says to Ben, as if apologizing.

Ben shrugs and hands her the ball.

Dimario is sitting in a wagon, his hands full of blue crumbs from the texturized mat that covers the playground. He has a twig in his mouth.

What are you doing? she asks.

I'm smokin weed, he says. He starts sifting through the blue crumbs.

I'm cleanin the weed, he says. Man! he says. There's no more weed.

Come on, she says. Let's play catch.

You throw it to me and I'll throw it back.

They toss it back and forth and then he gets bored, throws it over the fence, laughing. A slope covered with bushes and unkept grass leads down toward another fence and then the street. The ball rolls down to the next fence.

Dimario! she says. That wasn't nice. You stay right here, I want to talk to you after I get the ball.

She walks around to the gate, descends into the bushes. There are beer cans and bottles and chip bags littering the area. Broken glass, cigarette butts, condoms. At the bottom of the hill are some school assignments blown against the fence. They have been wet by the rain, but dried out. The first has the name of a third grade teacher on it and is titled Crayfish Behavior. *What happened when you observed the crayfish?* is the first question. *They died* is printed in a child's scrawl and the answers to the rest of the questions are blank.

The next two papers have the name Carlos printed neatly in the upper right-hand corner and under that the name Mr. Streyfeller. They seem to be reading lessons, Lesson 68 and Lesson 70. Lesson 70 is titled THE GLORY HOLE and begins *Mr. Hicks set four sticks of dynamite in the lower hole on the left.* At the top of the page are vocabulary words *triangular reechoed suddenly neither heading revealed.* And another list: *speechless sparkling crouched sliding scrambled downward downhill stripped jewels thickest loose whoopie terrible cough deposit aware brilliant golden showcase caught visible.* Lesson 68 is SURT GOES FOR THE MEAT. *1. rounded swirl almost burn roasting stirring crouched curled mighty hurry Herb Luke stream poach should jerk grease 2. Wants wander wash water watch 3. blister scared rustling howled growl stared sniffed pipe spit toward rising paw foam fern wheeze* and finally *Limping paw followed Herb* and *friends orange poke want.*

She wonders if it's the same Carlos. She folds the papers carefully and puts them in her blouse pocket, as if she'll actually return them to the children who own them.

When she gets back around through the gate, Dimario's nowhere in sight.

He went into the bathroom, says Becky. Ben's in there with him.

She walks to the open door of the classroom. Dimario is standing in the doorway to the bathroom with his shirt up, looking at the chicken pox scars on his chest and belly. Ben has his back to her, watching him.

What you lookin at? Dimario asks Ben. You're not a girl.

Ben says something quietly. Dimario continues his calm examination, and Ben says something else. Come here a minute, Ben says.

Dimario drops his shirt, moves toward him.

As a child, she can walk for hours without encountering even a shadow. The sun is too high. The grass shimmers.

The wind along the plain blows her dress against her body.

She looks at the flat, conceivably infinite stretch of earth in every direction. The idea of it unsettles her stomach. As if there is just one road, without edges. There is blood on the road and blood in her belly. She is just a girl. Deep in the earth the salt is flowing, liquid. Igneous rocks are the compressed remains of everything that has happened here, on the surface of the earth.

If she vomited up everything about herself, she might finally breathe. Her name alone remains, writhing and calm. A frozen writing that burns the air.

The wind blows through the tall grass.

On the bus, she sees things the way Carlos did. All of the mother's limbs, the legs of hookers and muscular biceps of pimps on the streets of darkness fill the frames with a fragmented eroticism. In the process of entering this world undercover, the mother's outfits get sleazier, she paints on more garish lipsticks. Even the boy, when he finally appears for a few pathetic frames, reclines on a saggy mattress in such baggy clothes that the creases seem to bind the contours of his lithe body to the bed. She flips back through to re-read his mysterious emails, try to figure out how they attach to this image. She rides past her stop, through neighborhoods that seem haphazardly constructed, or else constructed according to a secret ordering principle that would be apparent only from an entirely different perspective. People board the bus here, depressed school children mostly, but nobody gets off.

They'll let you use the internet here if you buy something. After she orders a peppermint tea, the idea of a hot, stringent cup of liquid fills her with dread. It's like the acid face of the sun. She can't remember how he spelled his screen name exactly. There are two phonetic possibilities, neither one the correct spelling of anything. She punches in the first to get a profile. The name is something fake, there's no age listed. Under Hobbies and Interests it says something about making the acquaintance of generous people. The personal quote is the slogan of a major brand of tennis shoes that could serve as a sexual innuendo. Favorite gadgets: Use your imagination! There's a link to two photos that turn out to be body parts: one erection, and one expanse of flesh she can't figure out what it is. The creases don't make any sense. She looks around the café to make sure nobody is watching her, and then tries to figure out if they might match what she knows of Carlos' body.

She checks out the second possibility. This one is interested in music and discusses popular entertainment in ways that sound much more like "a boy." There are exclamation marks and phonetic spellings and slang she doesn't know that could easily belong to a teenager. There is a cartoon graphic that's incredibly naïve in the extremity of its violence. If she sent him mail, he would feel like she was prying, but if she had to she could use it. She isn't sure what she means by "had to."

Her backyard is full of fireflies. She wonders what they are all doing right now. It's after curfew; perhaps Carlos is sleeping in Ben's bed. She ties her hair up and goes out.

They both do art. Probably that's how they met. Doing graffiti or something. They're both interested in drawing.

The night is cold, and the girls never look down. They just sit there, gazing at the stars. She thinks now that they must get bored; no wonder they escape, talk to boys like Carlos in the mall. There are always men here, slinking along, refusing to look at her, pretending it isn't the girls that brings them here, pretending their motivation isn't obscene. Then two of them get together, disappear into the shadows. It's as if a haze of misperception has been lifted from her eyes. She sees the street anew, and it's obvious what's going on here, what this place is. There were streets like this in her old city, there are streets like this all over the world.

She has to get out of here. Makes her way back out to the boulevard, enters the donut shop. The light inside hurts her eyes. She sits at the counter and drinks a juice.

A man sits next to her, starts talking. He asks her if she wants to hang out. Before she has a chance to formulate a reply, he says, Unless you're a good church girl. You look like you're a good girl. But even good girls have to be bad sometimes.

He's handsome in a way that makes her immediately dislike him, because she imagines he gets whatever he wants from people.

I'm not a church girl, she says.

Oh, he says. So you *are* a bad girl.

How tiresome. He asks her if she's staying around here.

Yes, she says. But no, you can't come over.

It would make her so lonely. She must become lonelier and lonelier, until anything—the least bit—is enough.

Can't go to my place either, he says. I got a daughter.

He expects her to ask about a wife. She enjoys caring so little. He moves next to her and whispers the position he likes to do it in.

I know a place we could go, he says. The Wayne, they'll rent you a room by the hour for twenty bucks. I'll split it with you.

Dutch Treat, she says.

You sure they wouldn't rent it for fifteen minutes? she says then.

He looks at her, not sure for a minute if she's serious. He smiles, altogether too handsome.

Ben is waiting at her bus stop again after school.

Friend still sick? she asks.

He nods.

They sit next to each other but ride in silence for some way. Ben seems preoccupied, staring out the window, and she doesn't want to intrude. Halfway to her stop she sees Dimario waiting to get on the bus with a large woman wearing a bandana.

He's bouncing down the aisle almost directly in front of them before he sees them. His eyes widen.

Hey! he says. What are you doin on the bus?

Hi, Dimario, she says. We're going home from school. What are you doing?

We're goin to my auntie's, he says. You know where my auntie lives?

No, says Ben. Where's she live?

He looks confused.

She live over by that store, he says.

His mother approaches and tells him to stop bothering these people. Ben explains who they are. She nods, sits with her back to them. She is so over it. Dimario is thrilled.

What's goin on at the school? he asks.

Same old stuff, says Ben.

You just left, she says. Don't you remember?

He furrows his brow as if trying, but lets it go.

You goin to your house? says Dimario.

In a little while, says Ben.

Where do you live?

I live over that way, says Ben, pointing.

Can I come over to your house? says Dimario.

Not today, says Ben. Maybe some other day.

You got a tv? asks Dimario.

Ben nods.

Do you got a bed there? asks Dimario.

A bed? Yeah, I have a bed.

I wanna sleep in your bed, says Dimario.

Ben is startled by his boldness. She thinks that he is exercising intense control. She wonders if he is startled by his own love, if he is unprepared for such a thing.

Not today, says Ben.

She wonders why he doesn't ask to sleep in her bed. She tells herself it means nothing, that children will sleep with anyone.

The man the night before was stripped to his waist. She unzipped him, but he kept his pants on. She herself was as naked as telepathy. He wasn't rough or special, but she'd grown to like looking at him.

Tomorrow you can tell Becky that you saw us on the bus, she tells Dimario.

Where's Becky? asks Dimario.

She's still at school.

She don't like the bus?

Becky has a car, says Ben.

Dimario considers this.

I been thinkin about you at night when I was sleepin, he tells Ben. I was thinkin about you with a big red hat. You was a fire chief with a big red hat.

A fire chief, says Ben.

Dimario nods. The image of Ben in an enormous red firehat strikes her as trite and ridiculous.

Afterwards, that man had stayed and talked awhile. When she told him where she worked, he started calling her *Teach*. He told the story of a kindergarten teacher he'd once had who had grabbed his wrist, and wouldn't let it go. She was crazy. She told him his people were devils and that he was infecting the world with his very presence. She told him that everything in the world had gone bad and that he and his people were to blame. He'd cried and cried.

Stupid beliefs had permeated the world, deeper than she could ever know. It had made her want to see him again, his story of being abused. But neither of them would tell the other a place where they could be found.

This is my stop, Ben says. I'll see you tomorrow.

See you tomorrow, she says.

Dimario watches him go, as if trying to make sense of some vast excitement and confusion.

Do you like cheetahs? she asks him.

Cheetahs? he says. What's cheetahs?

Oh you know, she says, they're big cats. They're the fastest animals in the world.

She's not sure if this is exactly accurate.

We have a book about cheetahs at school, she says. And if you want me to, I'll read it for you tomorrow.

You goin to the school tomorrow? he says.

We all are, she says.

Like clockwork.

The bus comes to her stop.

You live here? he asks.

No, I just have to change to another bus. I live way over that way.

Maybe you live by my auntie, he says.

Late afternoon, in her little backyard, everything is always the same. The still air, the mountains out there and the coming dark. At least she would always know where Dimario could be found. She is chilled, and not frightened, but terrified; but as if not yet terrified. As if feeling a terror that she will feel in the future, so strong that it is reaching her now.

There is a light on, but the curtains are drawn, as she'd known they would be. The street is less terrifying at night. She slips into the darkness alongside the house and around to the back, where she crouches under the kitchen window. A tv is running, but no people are talking. She waits there for the longest time. Just once she hears what sounds like a person's voice. What do you think of that? it says, or maybe What do you think of this? Somebody laughs, just long enough afterward that she doesn't know if it's the same person or somebody different.

At school there is a note in her box. Like the other one, it is written out in magazine letters. SURPRISE, it says, and includes a smiling face composed of disparate features. Grinning feminine lips, one brown eye, one blue eye, a nose, a dark mustache, spiky blond hair. The creepiest thing she's ever seen.

A figure down the hallway ducks into a classroom.

He was not the sort of person to show such restraint. It was in her own nature to be cryptic, not his; it must therefore be somebody he hired. One of those private detectives who play both sides of the game. The detective has found her and now he will terrorize her just a little bit and try to cut a deal with her. She doesn't have money to pay anyone off, although he certainly couldn't have hired anyone very expensive.

Maybe it's all a mistake. Maybe the note isn't even meant for her. It's a child's art project in the wrong box. She turns it over to see if there's a name or a room number.

It might not be him at all. People get stalked and murdered all the time, at random. This is exactly the sort of city where such things usually take place.

Maybe it's Ben. He realizes that she's on to him, and wants to scare or distract her. On to him? What does that mean exactly?

A legion of fallen angels. The corruption of beauty gives them pleasure. *Ben has all kinds of ideas about the future,* Carlos had said. They're designing a lush future of genius animal beauty and freedom. She smiles then at the way her imagination creates elaborate scenarios. It's all in her head.

But the note is concrete. Somebody wrote it, and it would not be the most illogical conclusion to believe it was intended for her. She could ask if anyone saw a stranger in the school this morning. They might have noticed, they are vigilant about such things. But the thought of providing a description, as if there's a person in the world she would expect to leave mysterious notes in her box, is too daunting.

Ben arrives, looking flustered and tired. He has a cut on his neck, as if he shaved in a hurry. The day passes quickly. She's distracted. Dimario offers to kiss Ben's wound, to make it feel better. It's okay, says Ben, it doesn't hurt anymore. She thinks he's being flirtatious.

Dimario, understanding perfectly, throws his arms around Ben's neck, laughing, and climbs him like a ladder.

Outside, every stranger who passes the chain-link fence could be one of his agents. Or one of *its* agents. It isn't humans who desire contact with children, but fallen angels and corrupt spirits. Ben is oblivious, exhausted. She thinks he isn't getting enough sleep. She could flee again, to a different city, but her check still hasn't come. She barely has any money at all.

At break, she heads for the teacher's lounge, but a man goes in ahead of her. His name's Bob, he's about fifty with feathered hair. He teaches older kids, wears button-down shirts that he tucks into athletic shorts, has muscular legs and athletic socks. That "coach" manner, calls the kids by their last names. She always hears him saying "control your body" to the children through clenched teeth. She can't bear him and the Coke machine just now, heads out the front door and down the hill toward the park. Sits on a bench by the sandlot. The playground is empty. Takes her pasta salad out of her paper bag and eats. The wind blows hollow plastic bags across the sand, under the gleaming silver slide. Radiant shells blazing and rippling. Someone is crouched there, under the play structure, smoking.

The cold bright sun. Melting the marrow of her misconceived skeleton, as if atomic, phenomenal. When the figure rises, it is Carlos.

Hey, he says, what's up?

Hi, Carlos, she says.

He walks toward her across the tiny littered sandlot as if a failed magician across a desert under the beating sun toward a mirage. He never gets any closer. He has a walkman on, his feet sinking in the sand.

I think I found something of yours, she says.

His eyes brighten in anticipation of receiving something he never knew he lost.

Takes out the carefully folded papers. He squints at them, already obviously disappointed.

Those aren't mine, he says. That's some other Carlos.

Oh, she says, I'm sorry. How stupid of me. I don't know why I thought . . .

Maybe it's Carlos J, he says.

I'm sorry, she says again.

She feels as if their meeting has gotten off on a bad foot, irrevocably. This coincidental meeting was so important. She wonders then if his name is even Carlos. It seems too generic. Maybe he's one of those boys who never tell the truth.

He shrugs.

It's okay, he says. How you doin? You up there at the school?

Yes, she says. What are you doing here?

Just listening to music, he says. And drawing.

He has the sketchbook open she thought belonged to Ben. The obsessive geometries are his, and she's confused for a moment about which scenarios and characteristics she's attached to the wrong person. Ben isn't an artist at all.

Are you waiting for Ben? she asks.

Oh, sure, he says. I was in the neighborhood.

She realizes that's her line.

You know Ben from your neighborhood? she asks. Or from his other job?

Other job? he says. Ben doesn't have no other job.

Oh, she says, I thought that he told me he did.

It feels like evidence, even if it doesn't match the crime.

Maybe Ben's a liar, he says.

She can't tell if he's angry about that possibility or indifferent.

I probably didn't hear him right, she says.

A lot of people tell lies, says Carlos, and she thinks that he wants to tell her something.

I do all kinds of things, he says. I like to do all kinds of things. I'm old enough. Everybody lies sometimes, you can't always tell the truth.

He sits, chewing on his fingernail. She tries to think of something to say.

What are you listening to? she asks.

Comida Mala, he says. You ever hear them? There's nobody else like them. They used to be more punk but then they started mixing it with all this Latin Music and it's cool. Here, listen.

He bends one earphone out and puts it by her ear, so they're each listening to one side and their heads are squeezed together. It sounds like a million other bands she's heard, except every once in awhile they mix in some of that Mexican circus music, with the trombones.

Great, she says, taking the earphone away.

What time is it? he says.

I only have about ten more minutes of break, she says. It's about noon.

Ten more minutes! Man, that sucks.

Maybe he isn't here to meet Ben at all. She feels a sudden desperation.

Are you okay? she says.

Huh? he says. Yeah, I'm all right.

Shouldn't you be in class? she asks.

He shrugs.

It's a flex day, he says

She doesn't know what that means.

Listen, she says, if you ever need anything. I mean it's okay if you come here, if you just want to talk or something. I'd give you my phone number, but I don't have a phone yet.

He looks happy, although he's trying to look like he doesn't care. She takes a scrap of paper from her purse and writes her address on it, the two buses you take to get there.

And this is where I live. You can come there any time.

Oh, he says. He takes the paper, sticks it in his back pocket. He'll lose it, she thinks. Something has changed now in his face. She's lost him, she did something wrong. What if she'll never see him again? It's completely out of her control.

Can I email you? she says.

I thought you didn't have email, says Carlos.

Not yet, she says. But soon.

He rips a blank page from his sketchbook and writes down an email address completely different from the one she'd seen him use at Ben's. It doesn't even use the same server.

I have to go in a minute, she says.

You wanna get high? he asks.

No, Carlos, she says. I have to go back to work.

Come on, he says. Just one hit?

She shakes her head.

It'll be like a peace pipe, he says, looking down at his lap. It'll seal our friendship.

She's touched. The fragile, improbable idea of their friendship.

No, she says. Really, Carlos, I'd like to share it with you, but it's not. You know.

He looks dejected. He lights his bowl, takes a hit. She's always loved the smell of it, so earthy, so vegetal.

Just one hit, she says. But don't laugh at me. And don't tell anyone, especially not Ben.

Ben doesn't care, he says.

She takes a hit, holds it in her lungs like she used to. She blows it out without coughing.

You're like an old pro, he says.

He takes another hit and then she takes one more. What the hell, she thinks. It's not like she's smoking crack. A huge mass of white cloud is coming directly toward her, blocking out the horrible sun. What a relief. She feels as if all this sun, so close, has been drying out her skin. The emptiness of the playground is a little bit sinister. Oh, yes, it's like this. This is strong stuff. She'll be stoned forever. The day is looming ahead of her, slow and tortured. She remembers now why she stopped smoking. She wants to say something to Carlos, but she'll reveal everything to him, all wrong. He can see right through her. He's looking across the playground, but he's really waiting to see how she acts. It's all a kind of joke he's been playing on her. He's mocking her. She can't imagine she didn't realize how sophisticated his thought processes are.

The sun comes back out from behind the cloud.

He must think she's a pathetic old woman. He thinks that she wants to sleep with him. If he doesn't think that yet, he will, as soon as she opens her mouth. Does he want to sleep with her? He's digging in his pocket and then he's playing with his lips. Everything he does is so sexual. Everything is a message. *My mom says I'm sexually active.* He's such an incredible texture.

It must be a set up. He wanted to trap her in her own thoughts, catch her at her most vulnerable. The world is so thick.

Calm down. He's just a boy. A connection between the note and the boy is ludicrous. They are both, however concrete and entirely real.

They must be dealt with, one way or another. She's becoming way too self conscious and analytical. But it doesn't mean her insights aren't true.

She just needs to be alone and she'll be fine.

Oh, she says, I'm late.

Are you stoned? he asks, grinning.

She nods, trying to look as sober as possible.

I'll see you later, she says. Okay?

Okay, he says. Grinning so wide. It doesn't seem like a malicious grin. She makes an awkward little wave with her hand and hurries back up the hill to the school.

She can't go back this way. Her eyes must be red, and she must be so late. Ben and the teacher barely notice when she comes in, so busy with the kids. She glances at the clock. She's right on time.

Dimario approaches, looks up at her. He opens his mouth as if to speak, then stops. He's smirking. There's a threat in his manner. He's like a man already, but smaller.

I wanna go see the fish, he says.

Okay, she says. Hold on one second.

He'll tell on her if she doesn't let him. *She stinks like drugs.* But she'd need to tell Becky about this journey to the adjoining room. It'll have to be kept secret or all the kids'll want to go. She can't bear to face Becky right now. She'll just quietly take him over. She imagines Becky reprimanding her. Why can't I act. I'm ridiculous. Surely Ben knows, but he'll protect her. He has contempt for her, nothing but contempt. Dimario is staring. He knows everything she's thinking. He runs off to play at the sand table.

There's so much information, all the time. Body language, muttered hostility, passive-aggressive silence. She is always shutting it out. People use and despise and judge, all the time. Ben and Becky and Dimario and the children are constantly reading this information about her. She is completely naked and alone.

But this isn't what she has to think about. She's relieved. There are so many more transcendent levels to operate on.

She runs to Jessica at the number chart. Jessica loves her form and never judges her. Or she knows she'll give her the more important things she wants: she'll cooperate in her attempts at ordering her

personal universe, in the never-ending process. No, it's more complicated than that, but there's no real communication. Jessica doesn't see
her. Unless she recognizes her as a kindred spirit?

A minute is huge, a lifetime is eternity. That's what all the mystics
said. She's a stupid stoner girl again, discovering that all the mystics
were on drugs. What if Becky talks to her, what will she say? She and
Ben are competing for Dimario and they both know it. Carlos, too. She
is terrified of the ramifications. She is too weak for such a struggle,
because she is confused; she doesn't know what the competition is
about, what she really wants, what she believes in. She is hiding now
in Jessica's world because of her fundamental terror. Beautiful children
are valuable property. Stepfathers the world over recognize this and
extract what they can while they own them. All the fables repeat this
story. Jessica repeats the names of each number while she points to
them for her. We try to discourage the stimming, Becky had said. The
self-stimulation. She becomes lost within that concept, which is this
entire universe of actions. Becky is mediating a fight between Noel and
Shedrick. Sixty-two, she says. Sixty-three. Sixty-four.

Jessica is delighted. Numbers are super-meaningful, they are perfect. There are intricate patterns laced throughout. They are like glass.
They are empty, yet obscuring. It's possible to hide inside numbers or
to use them as camouflage. Clean up time is here, at last, at last. She
helps pick up the blocks, avoiding the other teachers. At the buses she
busies herself with Jessica again, then waves goodbye, praying that
Ben won't be riding her bus today.

Once she's on the bus, she feels better. Not so stoned even anymore.
This is the pleasant part. She looks over those papers she found. *They
died.* Nothing weird about that, no hidden meanings. The other pages,
however, are a spider-web of language, sticky and complicated allu-
sions, a trap. Like the messages cut from magazines. She is terrified
again. Her heart is beating so fast, what if her heart fails? Of course it
is him, here, watching and waiting. Did she actually think he wouldn't
murder her?

She is so tired of having this drug in her brain. She watches the
houses and billboards and cars, refuses to look at the other people on
the bus. Afraid they'll demand something of her. The sky is full of
slow cloud formations growing heavier. At her transfer point, she gets

instead on the bus to the Salt Palace.

The journey is a metaphor for her own mental processes, with every detail forming a map so complex it is like a transparency overlaying the real. There is a storm in the distance and its weather, its quick temperature change gusting through the open windows of the bus, from the front to the back, and its pressure drop in her forehead: it is clearing her head. She discovers by making a decision not to be paranoid, she can stop being paranoid. It's as if she is moving from one physical universe to another. What she's been hiding from herself isn't a conspiracy engulfing her, it's the possibility that nobody has come looking for her at all. That he really has decided to go on with his life without her. The only stalker is her own overly active imagination. As for Ben . . . what? Trafficking in children? She laughs out loud. A fallen angel corrupting the youth with drugs, pornography, and homosexual innuendo? So what if he was? Even if he is attracted to Dimario, it doesn't mean anything will actually happen between them. They are only accidents. By the time she arrives at the plain, with the clouds purpling and black in the distance, lightning etched through the mass like roots cording an angry sky to a masochistic and greedy earth, she is almost euphoric. The bus turns back and leaves her, the only one. The salt crackles. The sky is the only thing alive, genetic database scrawled across it in nucleic acids.

This is what's real: the slow movement of minerals through millennia. The Antarctic ice shelf. She laughs at the self-importance of her thoughts. Whatever connections exist are irrelevant. The world is only vast and cruel and beautiful. Whatever happens only happens, yet doesn't matter.

The storm never exactly materializes; it dissipates and passes. The lack of apocalypse leaves her spent and clear. She knows that her destiny is not to be struck by lightning; that destiny belongs to somebody else. The man in the bar that night had said that every one of us is given a destiny. Only one, he said. Most, like mine, he said, are loveless and trite. But whatever it is, a destiny can be accepted or refused. You take your destiny or you leave it, and if you take it perhaps the only consolation is the pleasure of at least having a destiny. As if somebody cared enough about you to inscribe it.

Somebody? she said.

Or some thing, he said. Maybe something blind and not even conscious weaving possibility in the traces of its excrement. Like a slug. That's why they used to look for their destinies in the entrails of animals.

But all destinies are tragic, he continued. If you refuse your destiny, you may be happier, but maybe not.

How that man talked and talked that night in the bar. He was wrong: nobody has a destiny. Not here, not in this physical universe. Here we only wander through these places erratically, we see the wind and rock and light.

She doesn't care.

6

The next morning, during Playtime, Becky pulls her aside. I want you to see this, she says. She calls to Dimario.

Honey, says Becky, will you roll up your sleeve?

There's a big purple bruise on his bicep. She understands, immediately. It is all poison and terror. She wants to take him aside and show him her own scars. Tell him that this isn't love. She wants to tell him other lies.

What happened? she asks Dimario.

I woke up in the night and was playin with the fire in the stove, he says. And Mommy hit me with the broom.

Becky has called the appropriate social service agencies. This isn't the first time it has happened. It's all in his file. They're on their way to his house right now to speak with his mother. Still, Becky's afraid to send him home on the bus. Becky speaks, quietly, as if she hates that woman.

That woman must be so unhappy, and Dimario, and there's nothing she can do for either of them. She wants to escape with him to a distant place. This idea alone makes her feel closer to him, and a better person, as if it has been proven now that she is one of the few who knows how to love him.

He might end up staying with his grandmother again, says Becky.

Would he still come here to school? asks Ben.

She lives twenty miles out of town, says Becky.

Is there a school for him there? asks Ben.

Becky shrugs. Becky's attitude is somehow hateful.

She feels powerless. What if he doesn't come to school tomorrow? she says.

I'll call the police, says Becky.

Everything is spiraling out of control. Ben runs to stop Noel from eating Flubber. The phone rings again.

Ben is speaking on the phone. There's no other way, he says. I'll get him tomorrow.

He pauses.

No, I don't have to. Priorities, right?

At recess Dimario says, Pick me up. She scoops him up, one hand in his armpit, one on his bottom. Not bottom, she thinks. Ass. The tricycles make a clacking sound, louder and louder.

She is falling and falling.

She always knew that time could open up from the inside and that a monster lived inside each beat.

He wants to keep Dimario, do things to him.

Is he even human?

Those endless days as a child she had experienced eternity. What she had come to think of as the world, a place where people did things to each other or went into hiding, was the opposite of that. The only edge of herself that mattered.

Jessica has always known that what the numbers hide is the faint outline of a destiny after all.

The blood is all over the place. Oh my God, says some woman. The teacher's bleeding! shrieks a girl with too many zippers on her jacket.

She somehow managed to let Dimario down on his feet, crashed into the cement on her elbow. The boy who ran into her on his tricycle is crushed underneath her. She unentangles herself, grabs Dimario.

Are you okay? she asks.

The other boy is crying and she turns to him, consoles him. He looks fine. Her elbow is a mess. She's a little bit light-headed.

You're bleeding, says Dimario.

I'm okay, she says.

He inspects the wound. Maybe now he'll kiss me, she thinks. He gives her a hug. All of this has happened before, or is somehow always happening. She's entered the Dream, where life really goes on.

She picks herself up.

I'd better clean myself off, she says.

Dimario follows her to the bathroom, watches carefully as she cleans the wound with water and alcohol and puts the Band-Aid on.

She is absolutely lucid. Playtime is chaos, but she is calm. I just hope Ben comes in tomorrow, says Becky.

Oh, he'll be here tomorrow, she says.

Becky looks at her confused, then runs to get the phone. The phone connects them to a vast world of insufficiency and maladaptation. She can tell by Becky's hushed and concerned tone of voice that she's talking about Dimario.

There is Ben or there is the mother with the broom. These are Dimario's possible futures.

They wait for the buses. The bus that carries Dimario and Jessica and Noel is always late, always the last to come. They don't speak. She and Becky and Ben. The children are exhausted, the adults are exhausted. It is entirely possible that she will never see this boy again.

She thumbs through a graphic novel in which a killer is loose in the city. The killer is likely demon-possessed. She thinks the proprietor of the store is looking at her with too much interest, as if he thinks she doesn't belong here. Any adult attracted to the lurid and violent worlds of comics is automatically suspect. Or perhaps it's just the opposite. As the proprietor of a comic book store in a city like this, he feels he is always being suspected of corrupting minors. He's afraid that she's some crusading do-gooder or mother trying to ferret out the distorting influences on her son, the seductive illustrations that have enticed him into a world of illicit eroticism and contacts with strangers. They have a new copy of her mystery with the mother on the cover wandering the alleys. But when she flips through it, she finds illustrations she doesn't remember. Here's the mother in a comic book store, in a seedy part of town. The woman looks crazier and more desperate than she ever remembered. She knew from the beginning that the boy was just the door into a journey of self-discovery, but it's only hitting her, really hitting her, now.

She composes the email in her head as she hurries through the streets. She will insist that Carlos tell her where he lives, because of some non-threatening pretext, although she can't imagine what that might be. At an intersection where nobody else is walking, and only cars are rushing past, she stops. She digs through her pockets, and her purse. When did she become the sort of person who would lose a scrap of paper? She doesn't have it. She imagines she hears a hissing, as of a deflating balloon.

She would like to throw up. She's always had that secret desire, but she could never live with the violence of a finger down the throat. She wants to rid herself of all this consumption and matter, remain as only the tiniest tube of electricity. It's the middle of the night.

There's something carnivorous on the mountains. Out on the plain the lightning had seemed extra charged, enervating the landscape and consciously rooting through matter from one place to another. It couldn't be something that was only following laws.

Over in the House, along with the plastic cauliflower, the tiny cups and empty orange juice cartons, were old rags, hats, clothes for the kids to dress up in, including an old Catwoman costume with a plastic mask. Dimario had put it on and run wild around the room, jumping on chairs, dancing and laughing. For a moment she forgot. Forgot the little boy inside. The transformation was total. He was a magical being, feline and beautiful and complete. He squirmed out of Ben's playful grasp. He hissed and arched his back and flung himself across the room.

Let me try! demanded Shedrick and they started fighting over the mask. Becky took it away and locked it in the cupboard.

If you can't share and play nice with it, she said.

But after lunch, Becky had given it back to Dimario, because his mom had beat him the night before. But he went to the House instead and played responsibly with the smaller kids.

I'm the mommy, he said, and Robert's the son. And Jessica's the baby.

He sat Robert and Jessica on chairs and gave them plastic plates. He made Philip the other mommy. He talked to them caringly about safety and nutrition.

They belong to each other, through damage and fantasy and play. She belongs to nothing.

An envelope is perched on the stove. The stove in the night was the site of Dimario's crime; he was playing with fire. The envelope is impossible. It was not there earlier, she could hardly have missed it. She checks the windows and doors. The window isn't locked and she sees that it could easily, silently have been opened from the outside. Maybe when she was in the bathroom. He would have been not ten feet away. But she's sure she locked that window, she remembers it clearly.

She opens the envelope carefully. It doesn't tear. The letters are perky and sometimes pastel. She thinks they are cut from women's magazines. The teacher has stacks of them at the school, for art projects.

Predator and prey. He'll force her to become lighter still, in order to elude him. He'll make her disappear altogether until every trace tying her to the world is gone.

I can find out what you had for breakfast this morning, that landlord had told her. He was eating a grilled cheese sandwich. Crumbs and grease on his lips.

Maybe he's found her, but maybe she's not what he thinks anymore. He doesn't know what face he'll find. He'll be staring right at her, and won't even know who she is.

She is not afraid to look out her window. There are more helicopters in the sky and the moon is obscured.

Fuck you, she whispers to the night.

She turns on the gas. The front burner hisses for a moment and then ignites. She touches the letter to the flame. It catches briefly and then smolders. She relights it. Then she burns the envelope.

7

Ben isn't here yet. She should have known he'd strike first. He's taken Dimario and neither of them will ever be seen again. He's fled to the wilderness—some other innocent city out there in America where nobody suspects what you can do with a boy.

Dimario will need to be punished and Ben will punish him. And after he is punished he'll need to be consoled. That is how it works. She knows the pattern.

Becky just sits there at the table cutting out circle shapes for some fucking art project. She practices speaking in her head, so she doesn't sound hysterical when the words come out.

Shouldn't the buses be here?

Becky is rushed and distracted as usual.

Let them sit a minute, she says. I need to finish these noses. We'll see if Ben gets here or if they send a sub.

I'll go ahead, she says.

Hold on, says Becky. I'm coming.

The bus is too small to have him inside it.

He steps off the bus like a movie star, wearing shades.

T'dow, he says.

Nice sunglasses, Dimario, she says. Where'd you get them?

They're mine, he says.

I'll tell you a secret, she says. See? I have sunglasses too.

Put them on! he says.

Mine! says Shedrick, and snatches the glasses off Dimario's face. Dimario grabs them back and whacks Shedrick. She takes the glasses, sticks them in the pocket of her sweater.

They're mine, whines Shedrick. I gave them to him.

Did you give them to keep or just to wear for a little bit?

Just a little bit, he says.

Uh-uh, says Dimario. He gave em to me.

Well I'll keep them for now, she says. If they're going to cause a fight.

Because Ben isn't there, she must supervise the boys in the bathroom. Dimario drops his pants to his ankles to use the urinal. She thinks that he shows this to Ben every day; that the sight of it fills him with a vast emptiness. The squarish little butt seems less sexual than when it lies hidden in pants. Clothed, it can seem adult, but miniature. Now it seems dry, unfinished. He turns, pulls up his pants, with a studied indifference, as if pretending he doesn't realize he's being watched.

At break, during recess, she sits in the classroom by the window, watching.

A playground is the most melancholy thing. Like footsteps on the moon. The exhaustion of all that vigilance. Flag still flapping in the wind. Every day, the wind. They play and they play, always the same, just running in circles, sliding and climbing and biting and digging in the sand. You would think they'd get tired of it. Even as a girl, she knew that there was no point to such activity.

Pictures are taped to the wall next to her. A triangle by Dimario. A sun by Sharnay. A doodyhead by Dimario. A tree by Dimario.

He's gone. She rushes out, hands fluttering in a panic.

Where's Dimario? she asks. Where is he?

Becky looks around, unconcerned.

He's underneath the slide, she says. With Robert and Shedrick.

He is whispering and laughing. He seems to be showing them something, a secret. She thinks for a moment that it is some part of his own body, but then sees that he has something in his hand.

The last hour lags. Tomorrow's Noel's birthday, the teacher announces. We'll have a party.

Party, Robert says.

Tomorrow's gonna be a *fun* day, Becky says.

She doesn't know why people talk like this.

So he's still with his mother, she says to Becky.

For now, Becky says. But I talked to the social worker. His grandmother is there now, staying with them. Probably he'll be going to her house any day.

The buses are here, Becky says.

All but one, and they load the children onto them. She sucks in her breath, smiles.

Why don't you go on in, she says to Becky. I know you have a lot to do. I'll wait with these three.

Are you sure? asks Becky.

She nods.

Becky says okay but then stands there, as if hoping the bus will suddenly materialize. She shrugs then, hurries back to the classroom.

Noel sits on the curb. Under a cloudless sky Jessica runs circles around a tree. Dimario sucks on his thumb.

Are you tired? she asks him.

He shakes his head no.

Bus! says Noel.

In the distance it is coming up the hill. She pulls Dimario to her.

I have a surprise for you, she says.

He just raises his eyebrows. She whispers to him, then gives him the sunglasses back and puts on her own.

Are you comin on the bus? he says.

No, she says. We'll take a different bus.

The bus pulls up and the doors swing open, as in the song. The driver is a stern woman with red hair and glasses.

Here's Noel, she says, and helps him up the steps. And here's Jessica.

She takes Jessica's hand. She is choked with emotion and a physical pain, as if some organ is being removed or transplanted out of her. She remembers the way Dimario played family, took such care. Jessica climbs on up the steps, away.

Dimario isn't riding the bus today, she says. His grandma's coming to pick him up.

They stand watching through their dark glasses as the driver buckles the children up. Jessica is at the window smiling down at them or at her own reflection. The bus pulls away. She takes Dimario's hand.

We have to hurry, she says.

There are children still playing on the playground and teachers who do not know her. They are indifferent witnesses to her passing. A little girl calls out Dimario's name, but he ignores her. They head down the hill, past the park. She looks for Carlos. A parent is fitting her child into the strap-in swing. At the bus stop, there is no bus coming from any direction, and nobody waiting for a bus, as if a bus has recently come. They have to get out of this neighborhood quickly. An empty taxi is slowly approaching.

We gonna have a party? asks Dimario.

She is thinking about money. The street is deserted and she feels as if she is in a ghost town, but that she is being watched from windows and rooftops. There is nothing but the gliding cab. Her hailing motion is fluid, predestined.

She gives the driver her own address. Dimario loves watching out the window. He names the objects of the world as the world passes by. She smiles to herself at having done the right thing. Where shall they go? She watches the meter of the cab, numbers flipping higher and higher and higher.

Is this your house? Dimario asks.

No, she says. That's my house over there.

Do you have a son? he asks.

No, she says.

Do you want to be my son for today? she asks.

He nods. The driver waits patiently for his money and Dimario threatens him. He laughs and threatens the boy right back.

That's no way to talk to a little boy, she says.

That's no way for your little boy to talk, he says. You teach him some manners how about.

She gives him his money without looking at him.

There is nothing inside the house. Everything she owns is already packed in her bag. It all seems to confuse Dimario.

Do you have tv? he asks.

No, she says.

Do you have a bed? he asks.

I don't have anything here, she says. We have to go.

Where are we goin?

Come here, she says. I want to talk to you.

He makes a mad face.

I don't wanna go home yet, he says.

She smiles.

You don't have to. Listen. I want to take you on a trip. Do you want to go on a trip with me?

He assures her that he does. She tells him that she'll need his co-operation. That it's a secret trip. They'll need to wear their sunglasses, like spies. She wonders where he'd like to go. He suggests the park or the toy store or the McDonalds Playland. She counts her money. She wonders about pawning something, but what does she have that's extraneous? She laughs at herself. Everything. Everything is extraneous.

Let's walk downtown, she says.

She looks back over the space she inhabited so briefly. To be truthful, she had never been able to imagine a future here. The thought that she'll not pay the rent overwhelms her for a moment. She thinks of the woman from the agency, Debbie, with her aggressive ponytail. She locks the door behind her, stands on the porch with his little hand in hers. She checks the mailbox one last time. There is an envelope with her name on it.

Why she came. Otherwise it was stupid; she's thrown away her head start.

They are walking downtown hand in hand. It is a wicked city, wrathful and stinging. It is aluminum and pure and frightening. The sunlight and the heat and the bright horrible blue.

The travel bag must make her conspicuous.

She finds herself in front of that bar. Almost doesn't recognize it in the daylight. A short man is standing in the doorway smoking.

She peeks her head into the blind dark to see if her friend is there. You love to talk about things that don't matter, he'd said to her. That's what women are all about.

The woman in my house was the most willful of any of us, he said. So she seemed the most crazy.

Your mother, she had said.

Yes, that's what they call them, he said. She turned our house into a place where certain things wouldn't be allowed to exist. Men, basically. The men got back at her by declaring the things she said didn't matter.

It might have been the subject of mothers that got them talking about that girl in the movie, the one with all the personalities. Horrible things were done to that girl. The tap was dripping and there were tools and buttonhooks. She would never be able to have children, never. She woke up once and she was two years older. She thought that she could have more even than sixteen personalities. Each would perfect a certain attitude, a certain kind of talk, but the very abundance of possibilities would be a way of emphasizing . . . a certain emptiness or silence or a future without selves.

But what if one of them, she had said to that man.

What if one of them . . . what? Hadn't she asked him about the rebel angels? He'd rolled his eyes.

The rebel angels, he said. Quack, quack, quack.

When she opens the door a swath of light splits the dark, but the bartender doesn't turn. He is the only person inside, standing with one hand on his hip, watching the overhead tv. The sound is off, but women are swimming. The color of the pool water is celestial and impossible, like an eye. It is nauseating, although the cool dark is a relief. When she reemerges the bright hurts her eyes.

Dimario asks her for a juice. She stands there looking anxiously for a corner store.

I know who you are, says the man in the doorway. I saw your picture in the paper.

She squints at him. He is hateful and insane.

That's impossible, she says. They didn't even show that woman's picture in the paper.

She remembers that that isn't exactly true.

You don't know what you're talking about, she says. I look nothing like that woman. That woman had short hair.

Come on, Dimario, she says. We'll get that juice.

She grabs his arm a little too hard.

Ow! he says. You're hurtin my bruise.

Oh, baby, she says, I'm sorry, I forgot.

You're hurtin my bruise, he says, even though she's let go. She thinks that he likes to say the word bruise. She lifts him into her free arm and hurries down the street, past the comic book store. Carlos is standing just inside, looking at a magazine, and she stops. He meets her gaze and it isn't Carlos at all, just some generic boy.

I'll find a store to get you a juice, she says.

That little man is looking after them, grinning wickedly. She rounds the corner.

There's a store, says Dimario.

A police car is parked out front.

She was in a police station once. It was not life. It was all jaw and swagger and paper and fluorescent lights. Like a school. It was ludicrous. Crackling voices over intercoms, silly codes to make the irrelevance seem like mystery.

That store doesn't have any juice, she says.

Can I have a fruit rollup?

Come on, she says. I know where.

She heads the opposite direction.

Why don't they have any juice? he asks. Did they drink up all the juice?

The KK always has juice, he says.

I don't know what you're talking about, she says.

Why is you mad?

I'm not mad at you, baby. I love you.

Yessir. You is mad. You eyes is mad.

I'm sorry, she says, kissing his forehead. We'll have fun now. I promise.

She sets him down. Why does she say such things?

I can walk now, he says.

They walk five long blocks in the blazing sun before they come to a store. She buys two juices, gives him one, sticks the other in her sweater pocket. The cashier's broad face is like a moon.

What a cute little boy, he says, but there's threat in his tone. Dimario looks frightened by the man, but then smiles up at him.

They drank up all the juice at the other store, he says.

You don't have the blue juice, he says. The KK has the blue juice.

What's your name? the man asks.

Dimario.

The clerk looks up at her, addresses her directly.

We adopted a little black girl, he says. Just about his age. She's five.

I'm sure you love your daughter very much, she says. She wonders if he can smell the bile in her belly. How did she come to be here? These people are barbarians.

Her mother was only fifteen, he says. She couldn't raise that baby.

Did you take me cuz Mommy hit me with the broom?

Come on honey, she says and takes his hand.

The sun still bright makes her dizzy. Daylight is a poison here, all the eyes and police cars. This can't go on.

She kneels down to look the boy full on in the face. She takes off her sunglasses and then his. He is chewing on his lip and looking away as if about to be scolded.

I'm not mad at you, she says. I want to take care of you.

I promise I'll never hurt you, she says.

He nods.

Is it okay if you stay with me for awhile? Your mommy has some problems I think and can't take care of you the right way now.

I know, says Dimario, nodding gravely.

Does my mommy still love me?

She loves you very much, she says.

Saying this reassures her that she is not like that man in the store, that cashier.

Why are you crying?

He puts his fingers in her hair, brushes them through. They are so soft and so graceful.

Don't cry, he says.

Where does your mommy live?

Far away, she says.

Are we goin to visit your mommy?

She stands, brushes herself off. Cars are streaming down the boulevard.

I don't wanna wear the glasses anymore, he says.

That's okay, she says. You don't have to.

Can I hold the glasses?

She must not think about the future now. Everything will change. It is too terrible, too raw, too amazing. Someday she will wake up in whatever bed, whatever room, and for those first few minutes she will be disoriented. She won't know who she is or where she is. All that will have been dispersed. She could be the only human left on a parched and ruined earth, an obliterated and windswept earth.

They have to get off this street. A clock high in the brightness tells her how late it is.

She checks them into the Wayne. The desk clerk recognizes her with a practiced indifference. Curls his lip at Dimario as if he had been spawned here illicitly the other night. She is floating.

The boy's not free, the clerk says. Two and under they're free, but that big he's five dollars.

He's looking at her as if asking a question. As if suggesting she just leave Dimario in the street, collect him again in the morning.

Do they have swimming? asks Dimario as they wait for the elevator.

Elevator's broken, says the clerk. Have to take the stairs.

Do they have tv? asks Dimario.

Tv's extra, says the man.

The only window in the room looks into a light-well. Thin green curtains are drawn over it, as if it actually offered light. The thin mattress is a wreck. The chair is peeling, a refugee from some kitchen long ago. Dimario is watching cartoons.

When she was a girl she would run and run. The heat was in her hair and in her dress. The wheat was blowing. The planet was turning to face the west.

In the dark and stained mirror she's a mess. The reflection of the room reveals it as the sort of place a crime occurs in, walls smeared with excrement and blood. She reads the letter again. One of the W's has fallen off. She searches the carpet for it absently as if it is necessary to make sense of things. She asks Dimario to show her his watch. It is not yet time for him to be here. I won't be late, his message promised. He had suggested that she not be late either. But she is early.

Cartoon characters are blowing each other up, and Dimario is laughing. For a moment she thinks that he is mean, he is just mean and selfish, but then he looks at her and smiles. She hugs him. He gets up and starts walking around the room. He jumps on the bed.

Dimario, she says.

He looks at her sadly.

You watch out for the electrocuties, she says.

He sees the graphic novel in her purse and opens it up, tries to make sense of the pictures. She thinks he'll be overwhelmed, but the intricate images seem to calm him down. Evidence of his sophisticated aesthetic, she decides. He's looking at a picture of the indecipherable boy.

She is sobbing, and he is watching her sob. He climbs into her lap, straddles her knee. He looks at her like a stranger would. Ride me a horsey, he says.

She digs the cigarette stub out of her purse, lights it. But I don't smoke, she says, watching herself smoke in the mirror. The tobacco is delicious. She gives him the brush.

Baby, she says. Can you fix my hair?

They are always reading a newspaper as she leaves. These clerks and guards, they never look up. Witnesses to nothing at all.

They walk on through the now-deserted streets bleached and emptied by the unseasonable heat and the light. There are buildings in a turn-of-the-century gothic style and there is moon palace adobe with a hint of pink. Like the blood in a stomach or the moon drained of silver. The wind comes now and again in gusts. She knows that when a bad choice is made correction is required. She knows also that nobody requires anything of her: that requirements and all that business are a veil of smoke; that what you do or what you don't do is a hollow shape, a matter for the hypothetical debates of phantoms; of those who do not exist. Land Cruisers swoosh past slowly the long boulevard out of sight into the impossible west, and here's a muscle car, and here a station wagon, and here a Buick. An abandoned hot dog stand, and cloverleaf of freeway dispersing the traffic throughout the city. She leans forward into the wind, and it tears her eyes, and she wishes she were really crying. The sky goes on all the way to space and all the way to the north. Everything here is composed of the north and the west.

When she returns the room is just as she left it. The tv is still running but she turns it off. It leaves an electricity in the dark, a static energy of possible and unlikely image. The green curtain, the bedcover the color of a mushroom's underbelly. An ashtray that carries a message she hasn't the heart to read. The telephone book is torn and there is no phone. She reads the stains on the bedcover, the cigarette burns as if omens of her future. She is clairvoyant. The future is clear, and useless as ever. She laughs, and then she sobs. She stops herself. The pattern on the wallpaper is intricate.

She can picture the dusk out there, although none of it comes into this room. The stone buildings like a vast facade. The hushed and empty streets, and he is walking through them, toward the rendezvous. The Wayne, the note had said.

She looks through her purse, not sure what she is looking for. There are tampons and loose change and magazines and her money clip. A beautiful silver scissors, so heavy in her hands. Her mother gave it to her, many years ago. If she were ever to cut off all that beautiful hair, it would be with these scissors, but she will never do that. If only she could sleep. And wake, not remembering who or where she is. She imagines herself arriving in a strange city at night, hair cropped like a boy's, cunning and ready for the future. That woman had discovered that anything was possible. She turns back to the tarnished mirror. She smiles. She's alone now. The scissors are cradled in her lap. She studies her face again in the dark glass.

There's no moon here. The light-well is darkening.

Seen from the rooftops, the men in the street would seem to be the tentacles of a single organism fanning out to envelope something. But it is one man alone who takes the lead; his footsteps pad silently up the stairs, down the hallway. One man alone finds a door ajar, and enters. The detective.

Outside, a crowd has gathered. That woman over there, somebody says, that's the boy's mother. Somebody else has a bad feeling; there are spirits involved, lost beings from the other world. Several people nod. I heard things were done to him, someone says. By her? somebody asks. Or by him? What do you mean him? You mean with the *body*? someone else says. You've got it all wrong, somebody says. What boy? someone asks. Isn't it that woman from the news? Someone says, I heard she took a man in there, not knowing he was a killer. Women have been reporting close encounters with stalkers, somebody says. Several people nod—a killer is loose in their city. *Was* loose, someone says. Not anymore. That can't be the mother, somebody says. It doesn't make any sense. It isn't just natural, someone says. If they found a body, somebody says, it wasn't the boy's. The boy was okay. What boy? someone says. Somebody says, There wasn't ever any boy. Someone says, No, you've got it confused.

Inside, the quiet is absolute. Men step gingerly into the room, so as not to disturb it. One of them points to a damp spot on the wall. The detective moves toward it, squinting, but doesn't touch it. Nobody moves. He cocks his head then, as if he hears something. No, he shakes his head. It was nothing. The others don their gloves. They tread lightly, careful not to contaminate the evidence in the empty room.

NO TIME FLAT

If the earth is a sphere, then the abyss below the earth is also its heavens; and the difference between them is no more than time, the time of the earth's turning. If the earth is a vast horizontal surface reflecting, invisibly, even for each man his own proper soul, then again, the abyss below the earth is also its heavens, and the difference between them is time, the time of an eye lifting and dropping.

—Maya Deren, *Divine Horsemen: The Living Gods of Haiti*

Report 1
INVESTIGATIVE REPORT
OFFENSE:
VICTIM:
DATE: 10-6
IS THERE EVIDENCE STORED IN EVIDENCE VAULT: Evidence
has been set aside for DNA testing, a blue fiber or
possibly pubic hair. Clothing: jeans, shirts, tennis
shoes, blue scarf, underclothes, some CHILD's size,
some adult.

CRIME SCENE NOTES
Thurs. Oct 6th, 1:45 P.M.
Steve J. - Mike A.
Locate Body
-Thurs. - Oct 6th
-2:45 p.m.
-Body Removed from Creek.
-Body Was Nude
-Wrist + feet tied together
-Tied with what appears to be shoe laces.
-Abrasion to left side of forehead.
-Blood Coming from Nose after being taken from the
water -
-1 Pair of what appears to be blue Jeans from the
Creek.
Two officers are in the Creek. They are. Sgt. Mike A.
+ Det. Bryan R.
Also found in the Creek was a pair of tennis shoes.
OFFICERS ON THE SCENE
Det. D.
Det. A.
Insp. G.
Det. B.
Lt. H.
Capt. M.
Taking Polaroid Pictures: Det. B.
A Separate path than the original is being made by
Investigators. We are using yellow Police Line Tape, So
Not to disturb the Original Path in the area. Entry by

OFFicers to the Crime Scene Will be at the rear of the
Bluebird Motel.
Time: 2:56 p.m - Det. R - Locates bloody shirt. Approx.
25ft South of Body - (this is a Visual guess)
Feet are pointing up stream - (North)
PAGE 3 OF 6
Head is pointing down Stream (South)
Body has Several Wounds the left Side of face.
(possibly just
one large wound)
2:59 p.m. [this time was written in the margin and
appears to have been added later]
Blue fiber is removed from lower back.
Blood is Coming from ear. (left)
There is a large hole there where...
[next page is missing]
PAGE 5 OF 6
Sgt. H. - Notes of Crime Scene.
Sgt. A. - Recovered a Partial Shoe print.
West Side of Bank where Body Was located.
Near Body pair of Jeans were located. [the word "Boy"
is crossed out] baseball cap, child's size Located.
also two more pairs of tennis Shoes located by Body.
Left Shoe - Tennis (Nike) -
Black / Purple Shoe / Black lace is still there.
Pair of Jeans found is a Gap Brand waist size 30
Turned inside Out.
1-Pair of Nintendo Super Mario Underwear
-Under Shirt - White - turned inside out Located Close
to Body
-Size 8 - Coast Highway Brand
Blue scarf [the word transparent is crossed out and the
word translucent penciled in]
3:55 p.m. [this time was written in the margin and
appears to have been added later]
10-6 - Ken H. - Coroner - arrived on Scene.
Will I.D. body found also present was members of West
City Utility.
They brought to the Scene a Water pump and Sand Bags
so to Block off the Creek and pump the Water Out So to
Search Creek Bottom
PAGE 6 OF 6

also Present were Members of County Search + Rescue.
This Organization located the three bicycles which were
taken from under the Pipe crossing the stream.
OFFicer Shane G.- Drug Task Force, Was present and took
control of the Bicycles
-Det. B. photographed the recovery of the Bicycles. 1st
Measurement from the Large tree on the East side of the
Bank will be 14'7" from where Body was found
- from the large on West Bank, 10'6", from the tree at
the top of the Bank South of that Location is 18'8",
which is a triangle Location.
Body 27' - is the Width of the [the word "Stream" is
crossed out] Creek Where body Was found.
Width of [the partial word "St" is crossed out] Creek
is Consistent with Where partial footprint was located.

THE PROPERTY STRETCHED ON AS FAR AS THE BOY COULD SEE IN each direction, fields smothered with snow. Each winter was an ice age of its own; he expected someday to see a glacier creeping toward him from the distance. Instead, the sky was a damp grey rag and wind blew through time like a whip. Dead weeds and scrub poked through the crush of the snow. On rare winter weekends when the sun came out, the snow was dazzling and the property was commensurate with light. The boy was blinded, and the blindness felt true and deep.

Weekdays, he missed what light might come. He trudged in darkness down the lane and waited there for a little blue bus to collect him. He never knew at what point exactly during the drive toward the mountains in the west the property ended and the rest of the state began, only that the fields became less barren and then the bus would stop at another lane in front of another house. Wade believed that the wiry boy who boarded there was forced to dress and undress in the cold. Perhaps his parents had been smacked by robbers, lived in fear of the robbers' return. Through the endless ride toward the school in the west, past derelict trains and plateaus, the children on the bus never spoke. It was as if they were frozen shut.

THE BUS TOOK HIM ON FOREVER TOWARD THE MOUNTAINS, AND into a town nestled at their base, a town devoted to atmospheric research, the celebration of its now-defunct coal mining industry, and the promotion of the family unit as the organizing principle of choice. Somewhere in the vicinity was a military base, where men donned frumpy uniforms and performed what was expected of them. The school itself was dimly lit, and the tile floors a chipped and faded emptiness. Their color was not a color, and their design was not a design. Elsewhere, the sun moved across the sky. A bell rang, and the same bus drove for hours in silence back across the plains to the quiet home where Wade lived alone with his mother and father. The sun would have set behind the mountains, and the property would lie only in shadow.

HIS PARENTS WERE OLD; THEIR OTHER CHILDREN HAD GROWN and gone off into the world. He had dim memories of these brothers and sisters but wasn't sure if the memories were memories of the actual persons, or just memories of his flimsy set of facts. Their rooms lay empty, cluttered with clothes and fabrics, old magazines, exiled furniture, unfixed minor appliances. Wade wasn't there to keep up the farm in his parents' old age; there were no more chores to perform. There was no more reason for his childhood than for pleasure or work. His father had simply quit and the land was left to the weather. The weather was bleak and fantastic.

LIKE THE WINTERS, THE SUMMERS NEVER ENDED. SUMMERS WERE endless haze of light and sky punctuated with lightning storm. At night he could watch electric flashes lighting up the horizon far in the distance, someplace unimaginable as jelly. On the hottest day of summer the sun was made of ice. Only the clouds offered something like love to a boy alone on the land, a fluctuating roof of twisted and tortured shapes casting huge shadows that crawled across the property. Wade had read about green seas, and about the end of the world where the seas poured off the edge into space. Still, no other place seemed particularly real or relevant. He did not doubt that he lived in the center of the world, and that every other place was a suburb of this. When he first heard the phrase "the middle of nowhere," he had always known just what it meant. He did not think of the land as barren; it was cryptic and impolite. The land: nothing was happening on it. There was nowhere to hide. But the opposite was also true, the horizon often shimmered. He watched with anxious pleasure to see clouds collide. A plane drifted across the sky; every time it happened, it was a shock. Every time it happened seemed like the same time. Like it was always the same plane, and for a moment, he was always the same boy.

BETWEEN THE SILENCE OF HIS PARENTS AND THE FANTASTIC changes in the sky, Wade existed in a world constrained by ludicrously out-of-date information. The house was full of books and magazines and encyclopedia, but nothing written since the end of the Second World War. Wade knew all about trench warfare, the pony express, the gold rush, but nothing about the more recent slaughters and accelerations. At school, the recent past wasn't taught either. The bomb itself was discussed, a matter even of local pride, for the town had, in fact, some serene and organic relationship to the bomb. Wade never got the specifics.

In the attic of the farmhouse, he found evidence that lust had once existed, in an illustrated story. The young soldier had to lie perfectly still for hours to avoid detection. Ants wandered over his body, biting him and sucking his juices—the most compelling fact of history. He wasn't naked, but grimacing inside a hollow log. Wade didn't know how to locate his excitement. On the farm there was nothing about hiding or ants or logs that interested him. He hid the book away, however, so that he could forget about it and rediscover it time and time again.

WINTER RETURNED. HE HAD BEEN TRAPPED AND ALONE IN A childhood forever. He was at the mercy of space and cold. One evening in the middle of a blizzard, he wrapped himself in his mittens and snowpants and lay outside in a large snowbank, waiting for the snow to erase him completely. It was surprisingly warm in the snowbank, and his mind filled with a pleasing geometry of filmy light.

Through the noise of the wind a car engine groaned. Two circles of blurred light crawled down the road through the storm. Just before the lane, the lights veered off the road as if swatted into a snowbank. The engine shut off. A blobby creature emerged, and waddled toward the house.

In the living room his parents woke from their dozing, slowly rose, peered into the dark, and welcomed the shape into their home. Wade had never witnessed such hospitality; they stood chatting and smiling as if it was the most natural thing in the world for a traveler to find refuge there from the storm. The shape began to peel off its layers and Wade drew closer to the window to see, until he was standing with his face nearly pressed against the glass. It was the most beautiful human Wade had ever seen, smooth skin and black hair cropped close to his head in swirls, sweat gleaming on his forehead and his upper lip.

WADE UNDRESSED IN HIS ROOM, LISTENING TO THE HOT WATER run into the tub across the hall. Wade thought the traveler was having an adventure, that he had betrayed his home and family in order to wander the earth. He thought if he could see that man naked it would nourish him for the rest of his life.

The bathroom door was cracked and Wade stood just outside. An ankle hung over the edge of the tub. His father was now shuffling and wheezing up the stairs, and Wade stepped back into the doorway of his room. His father carried a neatly folded towel; Wade blocked the old man's path and held out his hands to take it. Wade discovered in this way that he wanted something and that he could bend the world to his will. His father hadn't ever understood or even wondered about the motivations of this son; he refused now to even see his boy, but relinquished the towel.

Wade carefully draped it over the towel rack and smoothed it out. The stranger smiled at Wade, and kept him there, asking questions, completely comfortable with the nakedness that wavered beneath the steaming water of the tub. The man was curious about Wade's likes and dislikes.

I don't like bananas, Wade told him.

His favorite color was blue. His favorite weather was lightning.

Good, the man said. You've pieced together a story with no external logic. You must be adamant about your choices.

Wade wanted to give him something special, a butterfly or a game, but he was terribly certain that nothing was special.

More than learning to get along with the others, the man said, what's important is creating a unique . . .

He wove his hand through space as if gently trapping a flower.

Fragment, he said. A unique perspective on a shifting arrangement of facts. Or an inexpressible sensation relevant to matter.

Wade knew just what he meant. He imagined dropping something into the water, reaching in to retrieve it. He was suspended somewhere new and different, yet it wasn't what he thought. He was greedy for more. He hadn't yet seen the man's butt, although the man's face, smooth with insane tender lips seemed like more than he could bear.

The risk is that no one will recognize that fragment, the stranger told him. But we have to be larger than that, don't we? We have to dispense with something as distracting as hope or solace.

The man pursed his lips, as if thinking.

WADE JUST STARED AT THE SURFACE OF THE WATER, WHICH WAS
unperturbed. He turned and again smoothed the towel. The man's eyes
caught him in the mirror. Wade was shocked. His home was larger than
he'd realized, dangerous and fated.

You like swimming? the man asked. Is there a creek or a stream you
go to?

Wade forgot that he could lie; he said that he couldn't swim. Later,
when he walked along the dry gully on the property, he would think
of it as a stream or a creek.

Oh, said the man. If I was to stay around here, I'd have to teach you
myself.

He closed his eyes and sank deeper into the tub. Wade left the door
cracked open and waited in his room.

HE WOKE FROM HIS TRANCE WHEN WET FEET SLAPPED THE BATH-room floor. The man's beauty would have to be a secret, for otherwise it would tear a chasm in the earth. The man glided downstairs to say goodnight to Wade's parents. His bedroom had belonged to Wade's brother. Wade wondered if this man was, in fact, his brother. He'd seen pictures, but it was all so far away. Or maybe people changed.

HE LAY AWAKE IN THE BED, THINKING THAT THE MAN WOULD get hungry in the night, and go down to the kitchen, where Wade could offer himself as a snack. If the man devoured him, Wade thought he would sleep forever in the snow and be dreaming inside the man.

The kitchen was luminous. Wade believed that the most boring place had become a complicated angel. He pretended that this man had been looking for him; that he had been hiding and now he was found. He poured a glass of milk, which was like liquid light and snow and carried it up to the man. The man sat up from under the covers and he was sweating. His top was unbuttoned; Wade could see the nipples. A person was a creature, startling and alive.

How old was Wade? What did he like to do? The man said he had read stories in which travelers spent the night in houses where madness reigned, and he laughed, he put his hand on Wade's head and ruffled the hair and he laughed again softly but not in a mean way and said that Wade was a shy boy. He called Wade that, Shyboy, and he moved his hand down Wade's back until it cupped Wade's butt and squeezed gently as he leaned forward and kissed Wade softly on the lips. Backed up and said *mmmmmm* as if he had tasted something delicious. Said then that it was just like all those jokes except it wasn't the farmer's daughter. Wade wrapped his lips around the man's finger, sucking gently.

Oh, that's a very nice thing to do for someone, the man said. But you must be selective.

The man asked Wade when his birthday was and without releasing the finger Wade told him the date. The man said that in eleven years on Wade's eighteenth birthday he would come back for him and Wade released the finger and said okay. Now you go back to bed, the man said.

MONTHS LATER, WHEN THE WORLD HAD THAWED, WADE'S FATHER
drove him to a different farm to buy a bike. A uniform golden green
covered the land there, like grass. This was a crop. They stood in the
barn with the farmer and studied the bike in silence. The bike was
simply green, yet they gazed and gazed upon the bike. There was
some process of boredom and suffering in time required to facilitate
the purchase of this bike. Finally, the farmer's twelve-year-old son
came in. He was a teenager now, and too big. Wade's father and the
farmer went outside to work out the details of the exchange. Wade
blushed. He was terrified to be alone with a teenager, who had plucked
a piece of straw from a dusty bale, and was chewing it. Wade did not
believe that he would live to be so ancient and ferocious. The young
man chewed thoughtfully and lost himself in the pleasure of chewing.
Wade thought he was a delicious, impossible animal. He let Wade stare
as if he was used to being adored. Wade loved the young man the way
men's mothers loved them when they were going off to war. The young
man patted the bike seat with affection and an obscene familiarity, and
then sat on it to show Wade that it was just too small. Wade thought
that the sparkling green banana seat was excited. The young man took
the straw from his mouth and poked it into Wade's.

THEY CAME BACK A WEEK LATER TO COMPLETE THE EXCHANGE. The son was nowhere in sight. Wade's father had to sit in the kitchen with the farmer; he hadn't yet endured enough lazy speech to justify the extravagance of the bike. The bike glittered, it was green. Wade walked out by the barn. The color of the crop was beautiful and intricate. He waded into it and it was higher than his knees. It was varied and shimmering, green, gold, green, gold. He chewed on straw and walked back into the trees, where a small stream flowed.

Out on the land, he saw someone walking, and he thought it must be the farmer's son. As the figure grew nearer, he realized the man was too tall. It was that stranger; he had been following Wade and decided to come get him early. Wade stepped boldly into the light, lay down in the grassy plants, and closed his eyes. He thought the crop would be ruined, and this thrilled him. He thought the stranger would come and think that he was sleeping or dead, and touch him and wake him up. He thought that ants were going to bite him. It seemed he was waiting for years and years. He opened his eyes and sat up and peered through the trees, trying to locate the dark figure in the light.

NO TIME FLAT • 113

WADE DEVELOPED A FEVER AND WAS KEPT HOME FROM SCHOOL.
It was on that day that a shooting occurred on the playground. A sixth
grade teacher and a girl were killed and two children were wounded.
The man with the gun escaped, but was killed by the police later that
evening outside of Mr. Tippy's Hamburger Restaurant.

The shooting had been on a Wednesday. School was cancelled for
the rest of the week. The townspeople expressed their belief that broad
daylight had become more terrifying than the middle of the night. The
shooter was described on the news as a "frustrated loner" and psy-
chologists explained that he must have been molested and humiliated
in a school. They interviewed his elementary school mates to prove he
hadn't been the most popular child. When he heard the term "frustrated loner," Wade felt that he would someday commit a horrible crime.
When he looked around, he couldn't find any evidence. The clouds
had turned grey and fused into a continuous mass over the land. His
mother was napping and his father was napping and he was walking in
his tennis shoes across the soggy earth. The weeds with yellow flowers
and the tan scrub and the purple. No thought was a necessary thought
and no action was required. There had been herds of hairy animals and
there had been scalpings and outlaws and spacemen with bubbles to
breathe in and lasers and wind. It was all a vast ghost on the plains.

ON MONDAY, WADE'S TEACHER, MRS. AVERY, INTRODUCED A NEW
woman to the class. The folks in the capital don't think Mrs. Avery
knows how to talk about feelings, Mrs. Avery told them. The new
woman arranged them in a circle on the floor around her. My name is
Brenda, she said. She was large and maternal, wearing soft, nurturing
clothes. I'm here today to talk with you about some scary ideas and
feelings, she said.

Their hands popped up, and the children offered anecdotes of dead
dogs, dead grandmas, dead fish, cows, neighbors, people in movies,
baby brothers born dead, dead mothers and fathers.

My sister was stomped on, said a girl named LeAnn.

My daddy got took out, said a boy named Terry. The windows of
the classroom were so dirty that the sky out there seemed smudged and
colorless, grimy and webbed. Death didn't seem to Wade like a faraway
place. The idea that before he was born he hadn't *been*, frightened
him more. Fragments of children's stories drifted into his mind. The
screaming children, the bloodstains by the monkey bars, the strange
man in sunglasses. Some girl was talking about her auntie in heaven,
but Brenda steered the conversation away from religious ideas. Brenda
wanted them to talk about their feelings. It seemed that nobody had
ever before asked such a thing from these particular children. Brenda
had cards that showed frowning faces, smiling faces, each face tagged
happy or *sad* or *silly* or *scared*. This seemed ridiculous to Wade. He
decided to feel different ways, that didn't match those words, and not
to give those feelings names. Later, Brenda stood in the center of the
circle and wept. She wept for her sense of safety, for her dead friends.
The children began sobbing around her.

BRENDA TOOK WADE ASIDE TO THE BOOK CORNER. SHE WAS CON-
cerned that he hadn't been sharing, and Wade thought that meant she
was upset that he hadn't cried like the rest.

Maybe you could share some of your feelings just with *me*, she
said.

Okay, said Wade.

She asked him what he remembered about that day. Wade
concentrated.

I was right next to that girl, he said.

That girl had been shrieking and looking at the tattered remains of
her arm. The blood just kept coming.

The teacher came out with some wet paper towels, he told Brenda.
And he tried to soak up the blood, but he couldn't soak it all up.

You must have been very scared, said Brenda.

The man was shooting and shooting, said Wade.

He thought about his decision not to name feelings. Unfortunately,
other people's feelings were too interesting to ignore. Since he didn't
know how to discuss feelings without naming them, he decided to pair
traditional words in unusual ways.

The man looked happy and frustrated, he said.

Brenda nodded.

He looked like he wanted somebody to play with, Wade added.

Do you think that's why he was so mad? asked Brenda. You think
he wanted somebody to play with him?

He was mad and he was silly, Wade offered. Brenda looked puzzled.

He was sad and he was excited, he said instead.

It sounds like that man was very confused, said Brenda, but Wade
knew she was really saying that *he* was confused.

Mrs. Avery interrupted them.

Miss Dinkins? she said.

Brenda, please, said Brenda.

She whispered to Brenda. Wade knew that she hated him, but
Brenda was just annoyed by the less cheerful woman.

What are you getting at? said Brenda.

Wade heard the word "sick," and then something else. Mrs. Avery
shrugged and returned to the circle. Brenda gave Wade a hard smile

and patted his shoulder and left him there.

He remembered it all so clearly; that bloody, screaming little girl and the man at the fence. Somebody get her a Band Aid! Wade had yelled. At Circle, Barry was saying that he was inside at recess, doing his homework when the shooting began. Wade picked up a book about dogs on bicycles and looked at the pictures. Barry was saying he had missed the whole thing, crouched in safety under his desk, as they'd been taught to do in case of tornado. He had never been in danger; he had never seen a thing. Although Wade had seen Barry's picture in the paper, bawling and splattered with the dead teacher's blood, he accepted this new version as equally true. Nobody challenged Barry. Another child raised her hand, and then another child began to weep.

WHEN THE WOUNDED CHILDREN RETURNED TO SCHOOL, THERE was a huge celebration. Cookies with frosting, and a march around the playground. Shortly thereafter came a whole range of tests. The other children had to draw pictures of the houses in which they lived. They had to draw pictures of their happy time; they drew pictures of swimming and snowball fights, throwing things at cars, buying new things at the store, wrestling with dogs, and blowing up the school. They were asked whether they would rather work under someone who was always kind or someone who was always fair. Wade was left to read animal books in the reading corner by himself. *The cheetah leaps through the air with all four legs bunched underneath and its supple backbone arched like a bow pulled taut.* He read about coyotes and hyenas and elephants made sad by their impending extinction. There were fewer every day. Wade discovered a word for what had happened on the playground. The children had been *culled*.

Shortly thereafter, a new line was formed at lunchtime. This meant that Wade had to sit by himself even longer, while other boys with bag lunches waited for their pill.

The days were getting hot. The boys especially had become less interesting. They didn't seem to have moods anymore, or even a mood.

IN THE SUMMERTIME THE ATTIC WAS STIFLING, THE WINDOWS nailed shut. Wade found a periscope in the bottom of a trunk. He could now see that some of the stars moved and that some vanished and that some of the lights seemed to follow pathways in the sky. He felt there might be a set of instructions to the sky.

Out on the land, from a less devastated region, he first saw the girl. She was wearing a sundress, and had hair like pale straw to her waist. She was by a tree so convoluted and out of place, it made Wade think of some dilapidated hotel in the middle of nowhere; he had never seen such a hotel, but felt sure that all over the world, structures had been abandoned and left to rot. Some days she climbed the tree, some days she lay under the tree sleeping and dreaming, but as far as he walked she never seemed any closer. Some days she ran and ran through the fields with her arms outstretched. He could never see her with his naked eye. The autumn landscape took on the colors of a dying fire; the leaves fell out of that tree and then it was winter and she was gone.

THE BOOKS IN THE ATTIC WERE LIMITED TO A SPECIFIC RANGE of themes: wars, military histories, Americans adventuring abroad, good-natured murder mysteries, women and children domesticating the frontier. He looked through a book about antiquated communications technologies of the Wild West. He skimmed a book in which old women gave each other poisons. In the bottom of a cardboard box, he found the book he'd hidden there, with the soldier and the ants. He couldn't figure out why it had been so thrilling; he'd remembered the soldier more handsome and naked. Another story in the same book, however, was beautifully illustrated with brightly colored and queerly luminous pictures. He couldn't believe he'd never read it before. The story had writing and pictures only on the left-hand pages; the others were perfectly empty. It told of a band of musicians traveling across the desert. Their music was both intensely beautiful and magic, it enabled them to escape from numerous dangers and created fantastic scenery in the desert they traveled through; it hid them from the shadowy authorities who were forever on their trail. The musicians wanted to transform themselves into magnetic patterns and frequencies, but they suffered from delusions and amnesias. They weren't even sure if the authorities were real or a mirage, policemen ready to perform ritual operations, everything reeling and breaking up; the nomads would lose themselves, sending telepathic messages but never receiving. Exquisitely conscious of the textures of things, torture in the geometrical patterns of sand blown by harsh blue winds, bristling cactus, hair of the camels. Insects twist and turn in a maze of heat. Days of noon and nights still thirsty. Throats cracking like clumps of barren earth, they run tongues over lips; tongues are salty stones, lips crack. They test themselves, harden, prepare, but for what? Deserts multiply and shimmer, fade, evaporate, reappear. The individual band members disappeared, new ones popped out of nowhere. Wade decided that he was the musician they'd forgotten, although he didn't have an instrument to play. The attic was covered with a thin layer of dust.

THE NEXT SUMMER THE GIRL REAPPEARED.

Wade suspected that she didn't belong to any categories. She wasn't a girl or a child alone or a person next to a tree. She didn't know she was being watched, and so, for a moment, he stopped watching.

He could feel the substance of time then solid in the cavity of his chest. He didn't understand all this light, sky, anything at all.

The empty moment was not unpleasant, but he thought about that girl being chased. She would be captured, and something would be done with her.

As he peered through the periscope again she turned toward him and squinted her eyes as if she could just make something out. Maybe the lens was shooting brilliant flashes of light. He put his hand over the lens as in dot dot dash but when he looked again she was facing the other way.

IT WAS EARLY IN THE DAY AND SHE WASN'T THERE YET. THE SKY was dark with heavy clouds, the air thick and hot. He collected the kindling and he waited. As soon as she appeared, he lit it.

While he carefully nourished the flames with his breath, he watched the girl. She was reading a bright book, and he wondered if this book might have words and pictures only on the right-hand pages. She set a small radio down in the grass with the antenna extended to its full stretch and she danced. Although he couldn't hear the music, he was sure it was as bleak and fantastic as the weather. The sky filled with massive clouds. The smoke rolled off his small fire now and he began to shape it with the damp blanket into syllables of a vaporous language. The first syllables were fat and round and large, expletives designed to get her attention. While he watched her leap and pirouette and then collapse in exhaustion, the fire leapt from his kindling into the weeds dried from the long summer's heat. He just stared as if dreaming wide awake that the fields would burn and the fire would spread across all of Kansas and the sky turn black from the smoke, and he would stand alone in the charred remains of the state and the sky would fill with evil birds.

THE FIELD BEGAN TO BURN.

There was nothing to do but watch now, nothing but to back slowly away and keep an eye on the girl. She too was staring at the smoke that began to fill the sky and he smiled. The air rippled above the flames and the flames ran greedy across dry ravines and through untended fields. The sky blackened: the cloud masses churned and the smoke curled up as if trying to join them.

The temperature plummeted. The first drops were enormous cold knuckles on his forehead. Slowly at first, and then it poured. He searched for the girl and just saw her running away from him through the onslaught of rain and hail. He turned and took cover in the gully he thought of as a creek or stream, under a bulbous tree growing sideways. Lightning crackled and the sky changed and the earth turned to the kind of mud that is only wet dust.

[According to handwritten notes taken by Detectives
B. & R. of the City PD during an Interview with M.
on 10-25 at 9:00 a.m. (Her nationality is listed as:
American)]

"...Either at the first of this school year or last
year her son had set a couple of fires (small fires).
M. became concerned that maybe he had been molested-
-she went to the school and talked to the guidance
Councilor. She also sat the boy down and asked him
point blank if anyone had ever touched him. Had
explained to him that no one (underlined) touch him
where his bathing suit was. Her son told her that
he knew that and that no one had ever touched him.
...Thinks that whoever did this--the boys knew--at
least one or all of the boys."

Report 2

INVESTIGATIVE REPORT OFFENSE:
VICTIM:
COMP #:93-05-0555 CF
#:93-05-0555
DATE: 10-8
PG 1 OF 1
Talked with the grandmother of missing child at P.D.
she stated that her grandson had a pair of Fubu
jeans size 6 and plaid shirt blue and green when he
disappeared. Verified that none of the clothes found
at crime scene belonged to her grandson. [signed] B R.
10-8

Report 6

WEST CITY POLICE DEPARTMENT CRIMINAL INVESTIGATION
FIELD REPORT
TYPE OF OFFENSE: Homicide
LOCATION OF OFFENSE:
VICTIM:
DATE OCCURRED: 10-5
TIME OCCURRED: ?
NUMBER OF SUSPECTS IN CUSTODY:--

RECEIVED LAB REPORT ON ANALYSIS OF STAIN ON SEAT OF
BICYCLE SERIAL #13315678-231. LAB TECHNICIAN TYSON L.
REPORTED TRACES OF BLOOD TYPE O POSITIVE + TRACES OF
HUMAN FECAL MATTER. DNA ANALYSIS SHOWS BLOOD DOES NOT
MATCH BLOOD OF VICTIM, OR BLOOD ON T SHIRT (Evidence #
2161B)

ANALYSIS OF MUD ON TIRES OF BICYCLE SERIAL #13278976-
786 FOUND NO TRACES OF BLOOD, FECAL MATTER OR SEMEN.
WAITING ON ANALYSIS OF BLOND HAIR FOUND IN MUD ON
TIRES.

WADE GREW. IT HAPPENED AT NIGHT AS HE SLEPT. HIS PANTS would be too small in the morning and he'd bulge out of his shirts. His mother would carefully fold them and store them, as if she might yet still give birth to some lonely mutant and pass these things on. She would go into his brothers' bedrooms and dig through the drawers and bring him something large enough to wear. He was hulking over his classmates and now over his parents as well, and one day his mother went into a brother's bedroom and came out empty handed for he had outgrown even his invisible siblings.

He didn't want to be humiliated or drugged, but now everyone could see him. At school, he carefully crafted a hushed and amiable personality. He hid inside it.

In the time from one summer to the next he doubled in size and walked across the property like some newborn ogre now unclear in the relationships of heights, of sky and land and building and footstep. The burned spot was first a hard, blackened scar, and then it began to grow back, outrageously, lush green and purple weeds. His perspective had changed too quickly and so everything was still a blur. Gullies he could once disappear into now seemed like mere cracks. From his new height the land seemed riddled with opportunistic infections.

SEVERAL MONTHS BEFORE HIS EIGHTEENTH BIRTHDAY HIS MOTHER took ill. She retired to the bed. His father spent time in hushed, practically wordless conversations on the phone, as if information was being transmitted beneath language, in atoms. One afternoon as Wade came in after school, a doctor was closing his bag. Wade's father was frowning. The doctor took Wade aside and suggested that he go up and sit at his mother's side and say goodbye. Wade stood at the window and watched the doctor drive down the lane and turn onto the road and slowly disappear from sight.

UPSTAIRS, HIS MOTHER WAS BARELY CONSCIOUS AND MUTTERING. She looked at him sometimes without recognition. She was tiny and he was vast. His father brought up sandwiches that sat on the bed uneaten and then returned to a vague puttering downstairs. His mother spoke more in this one afternoon than he had heard her speak throughout his entire childhood, using a vocabulary he didn't know she possessed. Her head shook from side to side as if she was possessed of something she needed to expel. Sousaphones! she said. Too far to the left!

If I can see your nose, she said, it means you're out of line! Tubas, she said, you're holding back. She suggested they must march as a single living, breathing organism. It was imperative that they carry plastic baggies full of corn starch to dry their sweaty palms. The last thing she said sounded to Wade like *I don't love the earth* but he wasn't sure and then she was dead. Dead was a state immediately apparent to Wade; there was no room for doubt. He stood up. He thought he should call to his father, but he just stood there, as if waiting for something to change, although clearly the change had happened. He didn't know how long he was there before his father returned. His father's body began to shake; these tepid convulsions were a disturbing and un-natural thing to see. Wade was grateful when his father finally turned and went downstairs and out and walked across the land until he was out of sight. Although he couldn't remember it ever having happened before, the idea of his father on the land restored a sense of order. It was a desperate, torturing sense of order. He hoped that his father would just walk on and on forever, would disappear and never return.

ON THE MORNING OF HIS EIGHTEENTH BIRTHDAY WADE HAD HIS bag packed. Instead of going down the lane to meet the little bus that still insisted on taking him every morning, he sat in the low branches of a tree and watched the road for coming traffic. The bus arrived, waited an insultingly brief time, and went on. Perhaps the driver had recognized that monstrous thing in Wade that would someday just stop coming. Wade waited there throughout the day and into the night and finally went to bed, although he couldn't sleep for wondering. He never went back to school, for he didn't want to be away when the man finally arrived. Several months passed this way and Wade woke one night with the moon streaming through his window. It was clear to him that what he'd been waiting eleven years for was never going to arrive and in the morning after breakfast he said goodbye to his father and walked down the lane and followed the road.

FOR A FEW WEEKS HE WORKED IN A MULTIPLEX IN SOME STATE'S capital city. The glamour of the film industry was such that it wasn't necessary for them to pay more than minimum wage. You have to steal, said a girl with permed black hair and bright sweaters. She only pretended to ring up the Dots and Cokes, shoved the bills in her bra. The manager, a short, bearded man, came in at random and barked at the help. He was supposed to be off at the other theaters in the chain, but everyone assumed the bulk of his time was really spent nowhere, doing nothing—driving or television or selling some product or screwing some sad and masochistic woman. The boy left in charge was also eighteen, with red hair and a depression in his chest. He'd had heart surgery as a baby and could go any day.

He's an idiot, said the girl with the perm. But I'm not complaining.

In the break room, she always listened to music that was both plaintive and angry, a monotone with a twang that didn't originate from any real geography. This hopeless but energetic confusion was the soundtrack of her opposition to the city she'd been born in.

Take me away from all this, she said to Wade, and she laughed. She liked to pretend that Wade was a dangerous figure. Because she spoke more easily than he did, it was an easy game to play.

If all the films had started and the popcorn was made, he could wander in and out of the theaters, catching pieces of each film. They were all pretty much the same. They were less about stories than about a rhythm in which certain things happened at predictable intervals: the discovery of bodies, gunshots, people speaking in excited and desperate ways.

THE REFRESHMENT STAND GLOWED. THEY WERE STANDING BEHIND the counter, waiting. Nothing was blowing up, and this was boring.

Have you noticed that boy? asked the girl with the perm.

An unhappy man stepped to the counter. The boy waited for his goods behind him, and stared at Wade.

He comes every day on his bike, she whispered, and stared, not hiding the fact. You see it out there, chained to the post? He always pays for the same PG movies, but sometimes he sneaks into the Rs.

When he got to the front and asked for some Hot Tamales and a Dr. Pepper, the girl talked to him in a false, cheery way, and then she confronted him.

You come here every day, she said.

It keeps me out of trouble, said the boy.

He slid a twenty across the counter. Wade took the bill quickly, before the girl could get her hands on it.

Mom works across the street, he said. He made some vague gesture and Wade didn't know which of those ugly buildings might possibly contain her.

Her friend stays at our house, said the boy.

You don't like her friend? said the girl.

His name's Jack, said the boy. Mom's afraid he'll molest me.

He shrugged. He turned and stared at Wade.

Jack has knives, the boy said.

The girl reached out a finger and touched it to his chest, then acted like she'd been burned.

Ssssss, she said.

The boy ignored her.

You're like that guy in that movie, the boy said to Wade.

I'm not, said Wade.

No, but you're just like him, said the boy.

The boy smiled and walked toward the theaters. Wade didn't like that idea at all. Once he was around the corner, into a dim carpeted hallway, you never knew which way he might go.

Cute, said the girl. If he was a few years older, I'd do him for sure.

It was the warmest day of the spring. Nobody was coming to the movies. The red-haired boy was in the ticket booth, doing his community college homework. *The New Farming and You* was the name of his text. The new farming involved genetic modifications and large corporations. The boy had been telling Wade how most of the corn in this country had been planted from the same hybrid seed stock. Then some new fungus came along, almost wiped out a whole season's crop.

You need to balance the advantages of diverse genetic stock with those of homogeneity for maximum yields and security, the boy had said.

Now he was highlighting more important sentences with a yellow marker. Wade had a rag in his hand. If you weren't doing anything, you were supposed to have a rag in your hand.

Jealous? asked the girl.

I have to go to the bathroom, he said.

THE BATHROOM SMELLED STRONGLY OF GLADE COUNTRY LIVING Potpourri, which they were to spray liberally at every opportunity. That boy was alone in there, shoving tissue into his pocket. Wade nodded at him, and he nodded back. While Wade stood at the urinal, the boy stood at the mirror behind him, running water and splashing. Wade turned his head and caught the boy's eyes in the mirror. He'd experienced something like this before; his stomach felt punched, and time felt laced with hidden meanings. When Wade turned around, the boy was tucking his undershirt into his jeans.

Do you know any good exercises to do? the boy asked. I wanna have a six-pack. I know about crunches, but I mean other ones too.

Wade shook his head. The boy shrugged, untucked his shirt and flashed his belly. There was an oval bruise on one side that looked like he'd been chewed.

You have a six-pack? the boy asked.

The boy was staring at Wade's stomach, and then he made a motion like he was going to punch it, but stopped short. This gesture confirmed Wade's feeling of the moment before. The boy laughed at Wade, and did it again, and darted away, even though Wade wasn't moving. He said Wade was too slow, and then he was gone.

Wade checked himself in the mirror.

The hallway was empty.

YOUR TURN, SAID THE GIRL.

She gathered up her purse and a bulging plastic trash bag that seemed to be filled with her laundry, and she disappeared around the corner. Wade was stuck at the concession stand. All the movies had started. He was afraid she was bothering that boy, but when she came back a half hour later, her hair was blonde. She'd bleached it in the bathroom. He couldn't stop staring. She looked different, as if he'd known her before.

Where'd you grow up? he asked.

She shook her hair and moved to catch the light.

Did you grow up on a farm? he asked.

She moved right next to him.

Kiss me, mysterious stranger, she said.

He was so startled that he did what she asked, then stepped back quickly and looked around. Her plastic bag was just sitting by the garbage, stuffed full of clothes that didn't make any sense. Jeans and jogging clothes, a green jacket and a silky purple thing he didn't know what it was.

Not very satisfactory, she said.

She picked up a rag.

I wanna *be* the mysterious stranger, she said. She flashed the money she had stashed in her bra, then dug a section of newspaper out of the trash. He looked through her plastic bag. The purple thing was a shirt. The girl stabbed a newspaper article with her finger. Give me a break, she said. Everybody knows it was the parents. In cases like that it's always the parents.

She tossed the paper back in the trash, wiped down the immaculate counter. Wade wandered into the first theater. It was about a serial killer. Women into kinky sex kept getting murdered. The detective herself seemed on the verge of a lesbian affair. Wade scanned the sizes and heights of the heads.

The next theater over was action/adventure. A meteor was heading for the earth, and somehow saving the planet had fallen to a retired cop. There was a little head alone near the front, but Wade walked up the aisle and saw it wasn't him.

The next theater involved murder as well. The cops had to date a lot of women they'd found through the personals to locate the killer. In the next theater over a clown was lecturing a child. Your grandmother needs you right now, the clown said. In the fifth theater, some paranormal activity was getting under way in a lightning storm. A radio frequency was picking up the voice of an air traffic controller's dead father from thirty years before. Toward the back Wade saw a head he thought might be the boy's, sitting next to an adult. He couldn't tell if the adult was a man or a woman. He was pretty sure those were the boy's tennis shoes, rocking the top of the seat in front of him. The boy's had been black and purple with black laces. Sophisticated colors, thought Wade. He stood for a moment and let his eyes adjust to the dark.

THE NEXT DAY, THE BOY DIDN'T SHOW UP. THE DAY AFTER THAT was Wade's day off. He sat next to a fountain downtown. A pair of shoes had been tossed over a telephone wire overhead. The sun was so bright it was hard to tell, but they seemed to be the same color as that boy's.

SATURDAY AFTERNOON WAS THEIR BUSIEST TIME AT THE THEATER.
It was Wade's job to sit on a stool and rip people's tickets in half.

I'm almost as tall as you, the boy said.

This was a joke, because Wade was sitting down. Wade could think of nothing to say, but he liked the way this boy would say just anything.

Let me see how tall you are, the boy said.

Wade stood, and the boy looked him up and down, and nodded. He rested his hand nonchalantly on the stool where Wade had been sitting. Wade sat down on it lightly, but as if he didn't know it was there.

Hey, said the boy, but for a moment they just stared at each other and smirked, as if it had been a ridiculous accident from which they weren't sure how to extricate themselves. Finally the boy pulled his hand out from under Wade, with a vigorous wiggling motion. There were no other customers around. The boy told him a joke about some jungle tribe that gave their captives a choice between death or getting buttfucked by the entire tribe. The punchline was that the captive found death preferable, but that he would be killed by being fucked in the ass until he died.

Wade took the boy's ticket, which seemed like a magic pass into a world of pleasure and illusion far more complicated than the movie title printed on it would indicate. The movie the boy was pretending to see was a romantic comedy, involving an exuberant poor woman and a dissatisfied millionaire.

Later, Wade stood in the back of a dark theater and saw that the boy was sitting again with an adult. He believed it was the same adult. He wondered if it was the boy's mother, or if it was Jack. There was some mayhem on the screen.

Wade didn't know what he should do. He had done so little. That boy seemed to require something, an act of will.

A man followed Wade into the bathroom. Wade stood at the urinal and pretended to pee, and the man stood next to him. The man exaggerated the motions necessary to wield his own penis and glanced down at Wade's. There was more fluttering and staring and aggressively banal conversation that halted and progressed to the point the man asked him what time he got off work.

I'm off right now, said Wade. Meet me in the lot.

The man was shocked. He kept looking back at Wade, to check that he was real, or maybe not.

I have to go, Wade told the girl with the hair.

She wasn't surprised.

Are you coming back? she asked.

Wade wasn't sure. She opened the register and handed him some twenties.

THE MAN LIVED ALONE. HE WORKED FOR A COMPANY THAT installed sprinkler systems. He kept talking about someone, kept describing this person in details both elaborate and vague, utilizing his own code involving military men, the working class, and buddies. There were no words he used more often than buddy and dude. He exhausted them both with his talk and his blow jobs, but he could only get to sleep with the tv still running. An entire town of people had been arrested for dealing drugs, early in the morning, still in their bedclothes. All of them had apparently been dealing drugs to a white undercover. Lawyers were trying to overturn their convictions after the undercover's shady past came to light. The issue was also raised of who exactly could have been buying all these drugs on a regular basis if the entire town was dealing. Wade slept and woke again into the Home Shopping Network. It was all about diamonds and knives. It's not my job to rescue anyone, Wade thought.

Whoever rescued the boy would get to give him pleasure, but it probably involved murder as well. He examined the twenties he'd been given, hoping that one of them came from that boy. Wade woke again later in the night in the strange bed and realized the man had been talking about Wade all that time he was going on about buddies and dudes. It was all so pathetic. Why even be a human being, he wondered. There was something barely hidden and basic this man didn't understand. They were angelic beings compelled by a destiny, a destiny which had nothing to do with any of this. Wade wondered where he'd acquired such an idea; it seemed so extreme that it just might be true. His head was throbbing. The night hummed and Wade got up in a heated confusion as the man perhaps dreamed and dreamed. He got dressed and left the man there asleep.

Note: According to Dr. Lawrence P. (as detailed in
the Practical Homicide Investigation), there are two
general but distinct types of bite mark patterns.
1) Those which are inflicted slowly, which leave a
central ecchymotic area or 'suck mark,' and a radiating
linear abrasion pattern surrounding the central area
resembling a sunburst. The type is most often found in
sexually oriented homicides; 2) Those which resemble a
tooth mark pattern. This is an attack or defensive bite
mark and is seen most often in the battered-child or
spouse type of homicide.

The following information is from the linear Forensic
Analysis & Psychological Profile. Bite marks noted in
this report have been confirmed as human adult bite
marks by a board certified forensic odontologist.
PLEASE NOTE: THE FOLLOWING DOCUMENT CONTAINS GRAPHIC
DESCRIPTIONS AND A PHOTO PROVIDED BY THE CORONER'S
OFFICE. IF YOU ARE DISTURBED BY SUCH MATERIAL WE
RECOMMEND YOU NOT VIEW THIS DOCUMENT.

Time Of Death Estimates
The Coroner's report completed by Mr. K. states that
lividity (the red discoloration in the skin caused by
the pooling and settling of the blood within the blood
vessels) was present. It also states that the lividity
blanched with pressure. Lividity begins about thirty
minutes after death has occurred. After 4 or 5 hours,
depending on environmental conditions, lividity fixes
and will not blanche. It takes about 8 to 10 hours for
lividity to become fixed. This could place the time of
death at sometime after daybreak on Oct 6th. However it
is only one biological indicator, and no one indicator
should be used to determine the time of death.
The Coroner's report, completed by Mr. K, further
states that Rigor Mortis (the exhaustion of ATP in
muscle tissue, which results in the stiffening or
contracting of muscles in the body after death) was
present, but that it was difficult to assess due to
the way the victim was bound. As a general biological
guideline, Rigor Mortis begins about 2 to 4 hours after

death. And full Rigor Mortis is complete about 8 to 12
hours after death. Cold slows Rigor Mortis down, and
heat speeds the process up. When Dr. H. conducted his
autopsy on Oct 7th, he stated that 'Rigor was present
and fixed to an equal degree in all extremities.' The
time that the autopsy was conducted is not noted on
the report, therefore it is difficult to gauge how
far the body was into rigor. As a general guideline,
Rigor reaches full even distribution within 12 to 24
hours after death. Also as a general guideline, Rigor
begins to disappear within 12 hours after that, at
which time decomposition begins. Again, by itself, the
use of Rigor Mortis to determine a time of death, or a
time range of death, is not advised. A time of death
of any kind is very difficult to estimate given the
differences in metabolic processes between individuals,
given varying individual anatomy, and given varying
environmental factors. The presentation and stages of
Rigor Mortis and/or Livor Mortis (lividity) used to
make such estimations are not absolute, and should be
treated as guidelines, not hard and fast biological
principals to be blanketly generalized from case to
case.

Report 3
[The following Report is signed "B." and he is
obviously confused as to the month. In this report
he repeatedly refers to "Sept." when in fact it was
October.]
INVESTIGATIVE REPORT
VICTIM:
COMP #:
CF #:
DATE: 10-10
PG 1 OF 2
Approx 1:00 PM I Talked to Bobby J., Jimmy P, and
Rachel S. about what they saw on the playground on
the afternoon of the "disappearance." All 3 children
agreed that they had seen a "stranger" and that this
was a man. Bobby thought this man was looking for his
teacher, quoted the stranger "who's that woman with
the shiny hair?" Rachel insisted the man was lighting

matches. Jimmy agreed. Bobby said it was a boy with a green shirt who was lighting matches in the bathroom. Jimmy agreed. Rachel said the man had a red shirt. Bobby said the man had sunglasses. Bobby said the man seemed mad and Rachel said the man seemed crazy. Jimmy PG 2 OF 2 agreed. Bobby said that at no [the word "no" is underlined twice] Time did cross over the fence to the North Side of playground into the woods.

Approx 2:00 PM I meet with Mr. B. + Friend He started Looking for his stepson Around 6:30 at 9:00 or 10:00 he was behind The Bluebird Motel in the woods and Again at 10:00 AM on thur. 6 of Sept. Did not see any bikes. He stated he seen a green jacket laying on the ground. Did not see any jogger but heard a noise like someone running and breathing hard.

Approx 2:30 I Talked with Mrs. B who stated she was looking for her son around 10:00 AM on the 6 of Sept. in the woods behind the Blue Bird but did not stay long because she had a bad feeling about the AREA. Did not see any bikes or articles of clothing. Did not see any jogging woman. Mr. B was not at home at this Time. [signed] B.

ON THE RADIO, A MAN WAS LISTING SYMPTOMS. YOU AREN'T SURE who you really are, he said, or you don't feel like yourself.

If enough of the symptoms suited you, it meant you were a candidate for some new syndrome. A feeling of loss that has no referent, the man continued. The need to be invisible, perfect, or perfectly bad. High risk-taking or the inability to take risks. The feeling of carrying an awful secret, the urge to tell, feeling oneself to be unreal and everyone else real, or vice versa. Lost memories, or blacking out a period of years . . .

Wade felt that way sometimes. It seemed he'd been to some colleges. He'd learned things and had brief affairs with the men who kept up the grounds. But he could remember it all if he really wanted to. The man driving the car pulled over at a rest stop. I need to check my email, he explained.

Wade wasn't sure how that was possible. The man sat at a picnic table and typed away at his laptop. They were somewhere in the desert, in transit from one dubious location to another. Their relationship was based on an accidental convergence of two paths of least resistance. They were both too lazy to try and change other people to suit their own preferences. Wade wandered off into the scrub. A dry gully twisted around through it, and he could see how high the stream had been by the garbage that was stuck along the banks. Plastics and fast food cups and a surprising number of articles of clothing, shirts and rags and underwear, and bloodstained jeans. The desert was the worst place to hide evidence, because nothing decayed.

The land just went on. He was pretty sure there'd been human sacrifices around here, he could sense it. Blood had soaked into it. Blood was curdling and the sun was blazing. You couldn't see the creatures, but they were out there, waiting and chewing each other for sure. They sucked up each other's juices, he guessed. He walked haphazardly along the gully for some time, letting the heat and his thirst empty his mind. When he came to a barbed wire fence, he turned back. At the rest stop, the man was clicking his mouse and talking to him as if he'd been there next to him the whole time.

It really facilitates community, he was saying.

Wade guessed he was talking about the world wide web. This man thought everyone in the world together was turning into the planet's brain. It had become the source of a mild but nearly constant irritation between them.

Not everyone has a computer, Wade said.

The man snorted.

I talk to people in Kenya, he said.

The man's skin was dry, hair frazzled and bleached. He seemed crisped, a little bit fried around the edges, like an asteroid that had come through the atmosphere a few times too many. Wade knew that his time with this man was approaching its end. The sun was blazing out here and the electronic screen seemed grotesque. Wade thought there must a club of dictators or child murderers he was connecting with in Kenya. The man was wearing a stained undershirt and suit pants.

More evidence. Guilty, thought Wade, but surely nobody cared. He thought then that his mood was the same as America's, or he thought that his mood was exactly "America." The man shivered in the heat, as if he was finally ready to move on, but then he continued clicking away, a sort of hopeless scratching noise under the sun. There was a weird hair or blue fiber there where the shirt, drenched with sweat, was sticking to the man's back.

WADE HAD NEVER IMAGINED THAT HE'D WANT TO RETURN home, so he was as surprised by his own impulse as by the fact that he couldn't find the place. When he told the calm man who was his most recent lover that he was from the part of western Kansas where Kansas hit the mountains, the man told him his geography was impossible. They drove all over and nothing looked familiar. He was sure his father was dead by now. He left the calm man and spent weeks driving north and south along the base of the Rockies, thinking that perhaps he had been mistaken and had never actually lived in Kansas at all. But he found no town with its combination of military complexes and atmospheric research in Colorado or New Mexico either. He realized that he thought his father was dead only because he couldn't imagine the details of his being alive.

He drove highways at first systematically, but then randomly through the heat and the dust. The flatness wasn't homogenous, it was infinitely varied. He wondered if maybe that man had tried to come back for him after all, but had been unable to find him. That man might still now be driving the plains in search of him. Instead of consoling him, this thought reexcavated an enormous hole. That he hadn't been raped by that man was his only regret; Wade could have changed everything if he had more willfully seduced him. He would be living now on a completely different level. He didn't think these people would even be able to see him. There was nothing left in the world but space and time. The enormity of the land was a kind of innocence. It was so vast that everything became innocent and catastrophic. He guessed that something had been sacrificed here too. But the land was exhausted by the uselessness of the sacrifice. Children rode bikes down the highways, and he left dust in his wake. He just drove and drove and passed the same two boys again riding their bikes. He thought he recognized the one in front, that boy at the movies. He pulled over along the shoulder and looked in the rearview as the bicycles approached, and realized that the boy he was thinking of wouldn't be that age anymore.

The engine was ticking. The boy was wearing an undershirt and something else tied around his waist. He was dusty and brown, and he stood up as he pedaled and slowed as he approached. Those boys were the only ones for miles in any direction. The only ones with human language and skin. The first boy rode past him, made a face at him and wiggled his ass. As the second one whizzed by, the first one shouted something that sounded like *I'm available*, but Wade was pretty sure that wasn't really what he said. He let them ride on a ways; if he took off immediately it would seem sinister, he guessed. The newspapers were full of instructions for how to become involved with children. People were always getting caught after surprising numbers of incidents and years; their methods and mistakes were outlined in detail. The boy shouted something, but he was too far away. Wade wondered if he should return to that city with the theater and the boy. Suddenly, it seemed he'd been in love with that boy, although the idea struck him as absurd. He wondered if he'd actually had *two* regrets. He took off his shirt, pulled onto the highway. Because he was so large, people who saw him shirtless longed for him. This was a fact he had found no benefit in at all. His silence they saw as a place they could use. He wanted to leave the memory of his own body's beauty lingering like a ghost on the silent land. He pulled up alongside the boys and asked where the nearest gas station was. You out of gas? asked the more out-going boy. Wade wondered if the other one was on meds. I got plenty of gas, said Wade. Got a problem with my hose. They kept pedaling and he kept inching along beside them. He didn't expect them to get the cheesy innuendo except subliminally, but the boy snickered at his friend. The boy gave some nonsensical directions and Wade asked him to hold on, so he could write it all down. He wanted to get out of the car, so they could appreciate his size. He leaned over the blazing hood, and scribbled down the directions, which still didn't make sense. He stood up and put his hands in his pockets, said a few more things about his hose. Hey, he said next, what state am I in anyway? The boy looked alarmed. Doesn't matter, said Wade. He patted his belly and got in the car, muttered something obscene they couldn't make out, and drove away. He hoped those boys would fuck each other on the earth. He hoped they would just fuck and fuck and fuck. He hit the perpendicular highway and headed east again.

THIS CITY'S LAYOUT JUST MADE WADE WANT TO SLEEP FOREVER.
It was the capital city of a different state. He found the bar he was
looking for down by the tracks. It was named after its address, the 519
Club. Oh, the gays, he thought. The gays in the towns of America, so
willful and lonely. Drinking and shooting pool and lighting up their
tiny dance floors. The bar was nearly empty. Nobody was dancing and
then one boy was dancing by himself and then nobody again. A young
woman with her blonde hair tied up in a scarf sat at the bar next to
Wade. The men here are all monsters, she said. She obviously liked
the fact that Wade wouldn't say much, but would look at her while
she was talking. She was pretty, but not pretty enough to make up for
her perverse inclinations and her bizarre ways of speaking. They all
look like they're overcompensating, she said, for a profound lack of
life force. This reminded Wade of what he had thought earlier about
the land. If people want to be hurt, is it okay to hurt them? she asked.
Wade shrugged. He didn't consider this a significant moral dilemma.
She was so busy refusing to be a victim. He wasn't sure if she was
fooling herself, or if "ethics" was a kind of foreplay for her. Where did
you grow up? Wade asked. He thought she looked familiar. She spoke
instead of moon jellies, and he didn't press. She'd been to the Academy
of Science to see the venomous creatures show and couldn't get over
the floating transparent luminescence of the moon jellies.

She suggested they go to a local club and see a band she liked.
Outside, in the cool of the night, she was suddenly quiet. For a moment, in the deserted streets, it was as if she didn't know where she
could possibly be on the face of the earth, or what it could mean.
When they entered the livelier section of town, with bars and people
on the streets, she brightened again, paused in front of a window displaying dresses on bald, stylish mannequins. A sheer white one. Wade
thought: this is a gown. This is what people are thinking when they
talk about gowns.

I want to wear that and sit up at night in your living room, she told
Wade. What would you do if you woke up and found me there like
that?

Wade laughed.

During a thunderstorm, she said.

Holding a knife, she said.

They walked on. She wants to be scary and romantic, Wade thought. He was wondering if she might someday find a way to give form to terror in a less familiar way. She leaned into him, and Wade instinctively shrank back. I don't have a living room, he mumbled. What are you afraid of? she asked. He thought she was the type of woman who pick men up in gay bars, and that she wanted him to be afraid. He thought it was likely she would someday work with children or sick people or retards, somebody with less power than herself.

I like being terrified, said Wade.

She squeezed his hand.

But I'm terrified of men, he said.

There was nothing more to say. Inside the club, bodies were packed together in the midst of darkness and smoke vibrating together with the noise. The band's singer stared at him and sang to him. Wade became enraged. Although it had never occurred to him that he might be angry, he rode it into euphoria. The singer wasn't all that handsome, but his energy and extroversion were intense. He wanted Wade. The sexual electricity between them seemed capable of exploding the club completely. Between songs, the audience didn't look at each other or speak because individuality was a betrayal. Any settling back into human shapes would involve shame, which needed to be further obliterated before the journey could somehow circle back around. Without a direction this energy would form incomplete ogres. The singer and Wade didn't speak because there was nothing to say. Later they'd just ram into each other like men dying of thirst. Like men in the desert, thought Wade. In the meantime, there was a new song: amazing and then everything got weird. A girl collapsed and the ambulance came, but they were too late and she was lying there dead.

STUNNED YOUNG PEOPLE STOOD BLINKING INTO THE NIGHT
outside the club as if waiting to be collected. A freaky drugged guy
was kicking a brick wall. Three boys rode up on bikes, thrilled that
something had actually happened. Wade already knew that nothing
would change. The band had followed the ambulance; apparently
they'd known the dead girl. The girl who had brought him there was
sitting on the sidewalk sobbing. He was not the man to console her
and when he overheard a group of scruffy people talk about driving
west that night in their van he asked them for a ride. They said yes,
but still everyone was just lingering and crackling. Later in his life,
someone would use the phrase "a whirlwind with death at the center,"
and Wade would remember that night in the club and the woman's
corpse. Stop staring at me, said the drugged guy to the kids. Then
stop kicking the wall, said one of the boys. Was she your girlfriend?
another one asked.

He kicked the wall again. You need some anger management, the
first little boy said. Kicking the wall won't do any good.

Who says? snarled the man.

Your baby, said the boy, who you *married*.

This shut the man up. He paced then in smaller and smaller circles.
Wade walked over to a bench and tried to collect some sense of coher-
ence. He thought of titles for gay porn. Alpha Male, he thought. He
thought: Ruin That Hole. He watched as the kicking man began some
sort of conversation with the sobbing woman. It proceeded slowly,
haltingly, but then they rose together and walked down the street.
The boys followed just behind on their bikes and they all disappeared
around a corner.

The following information is from the Medical
Examiner's analysis of the missing child after he was
recognized by the clerk (David G.) at Comics Store in
the downtown area.

The first set of injuries is described as faint
contusions on the surface of the right buttocks (not
pictured). These injuries could be consistent with
the "parental spanking." The second set of injuries
is described as five superficial cutting wounds on
the left buttock (pictured on the left in this photo
at the right). It should be noted that these injuries
are actually lacerations, as indicated by the bridging
between the open tissue, and the irregular edges.
Both indicators are apparent upon close examination of
the photographs. It is the opinion of this examiner
that this set of injuries is most consistent with
the parental whipping. It is further the opinion
of this examiner that after having received this
set of injuries, which tore open the skin and would
have resulted in some severe bleeding, the boy would
have been unable to walk or ride a bicycle without
incredible pain and discomfort. Furthermore, there is
the existence of bruised ovoid compression injuries all
over this victim's inner thigh that could be suction
type bite marks. Bite mark evidence is very important
in any criminal case because it demonstrates behavior
and lends itself to individuation. It can reveal to an
examiner who committed the act, because bite marks can
be as unique as fingerprints and positively identify a
suspect. And, once established, it also reveals the act
itself: biting.

The following information is from the linear Forensic
Analysis & Psychological Profile, Wound Pattern
Analysis:

The shoelace ligatures used to restrain this HOMICIDE
victim did leave deep furrows, and also did leave
patterned abrasions on both the wrists and ankles.
This indicates that the victim was struggling while the
ligatures were in place. This indicates further that

the victim was very much conscious before or after the
ligatures were affixed to wrists and ankles. We know
that this victim did not drown, that is to say that
no hemorrhagic edema fluid was present in the victim's
lungs, or in the victim's mouth. This indicates that
the victim was already dead when placed into the 2? ft
of water in the drainage ditch.

Sexual Assault/Rape Indicators
As Dr. H.'s examination concluded, no sperm were
present in any of the orifices. There were also no
apparent injuries to the anus. It is also important to
note that though the victim's anus was dilated, this by
itself does not indicate or suggest anal penetration.
The anus is a sphincter; a muscle which is tight and
closed in most living individuals, and always open
and dilated in deceased individuals. When someone dies
their anus relaxes and dilates. The presence of a
dilated anus taken to indicate sexual assault or rape
is a very common misinterpretation made by untrained
individuals when examining those who have met with
violent death.

Lack Of Injuries
There is again a lack of evidence to support any sort
of strangulation. Dr. H. states that his examination
of the neck of this victim revealed no injuries, and
the photos that this examiner has seen support that
conclusion. There is also, again, a lack of mosquito
bites to this victim, which, as mentioned earlier,
suggests that victim received injuries elsewhere
first. This because the injuries took time to inflict,
time during which many mosquito bites would have been
received, even after death.

Report 5

INVESTIGATIVE REPORT
OFFENSE: HOMICIDE
VICTIM:
COMP #: 93-05-0542 CF
DATE: 10-11

PG 1 OF 1

Talked with clerk Sheila J. at Adult VIDEO STORE where
SUSPECT claimed to have been "hanging out" on the
evening in question. Clerk said that no one underage
was ever allowed into the store and that if any minors
had tried to get in she would have remembered. Said
that it is very strict in that regard. Clerk was shown
picture of SUSPECT. She stated that Suspect might have
been there and that Suspect looked familiar. Stated
that the video booths were generally busiest during
that time of the evening and that she had gone back
two or three times to discourage loitering. Stated
there were several persons matching Suspect's general
description, but that "back there in the dark you can't
always tell one person from the other."

IT CAME OUT THAT THE BAND WOULD BE DOING A WEST COAST tour and opening for a bigger band in a Southern California coastal town. That's where they were headed, more or less, but the people in the van annoyed Wade. They talked about music in political terms, and they wanted to have babies. They thought countercultural people like themselves would produce the best sort of babies. They bickered about things like which rest stops were most inviting and where to find the best bacon cheeseburgers, but on the baby point they were all in agreement. Wade pretended to sleep, and left them in Sacramento to proceed on his own.

The Central Valley was covered by a haze of white dust. The haze smelled bitter, chemical and fecal. The haze covered hundreds of miles, from horizon to horizon.

HE WAS DOWN BY THE WATERFRONT HOURS EARLY THE NIGHT OF the show. Two girls were speaking to him and laughing and then one of them took out a dropper of liquid in a blue vial and dispensed a drop on the back of his hand and suggested he lick it off. The sight of his tongue frightened them and made them laugh and they wandered off down the waterfront as the summer sun lowered and he just sat there immersed in some tangible minutes. The sun neared the horizon and huge black clouds formed over the ocean; the ocean seemed to be boiling, but he knew that wasn't literally true. He heard the news as if telepathically and he stopped and sat on a bench and stared at his hand which seemed deeply etched and alive and he heard it again clearly spoken from two girls on the next bench that it was such a drag that the show had been cancelled. He just kept staring at his hand and not looking at the girls who were speaking loudly as if they wanted to be overheard. He was sure then that these must be the same two girls who'd given him the drug, but now they'd changed their costumes. The more convinced he became of this, the more disturbed he was, until he looked at them and saw clearly that these weren't those girls at all. The fact that they were strangers and he owed them nothing was a tremendous relief and he began walking.

Drugged and disappointed young people were wandering dazed along the seafront and the wind increasing, with lightning over the ocean. The temperature dropped. The awesome storm approached in miniscule increments of time, creating a sense that something cataclysmic had always been about to happen. The disappointment of the concertgoers created an unchanneled energy which seemed doomed to a violent finale. The sexuality of the aimless crowd seemed aggressive and pointlessly aimed in his direction. He just wanted to hide. A car rolled down its window and the occupant asked him if he needed a lift.

THE BACKSEAT OF THE CAR WAS A COMPLETELY DIFFERENT WORLD. A man was driving, as if chauffeuring Wade, and Wade laughed. He found himself oddly comforted by the older man's aura of security. As if being driven around was the most amazing thing, as if he'd been saved. They ascended into the hills and left the storm behind; up above was a miraculous calm. The dashboard was elaborately blinking and bright, the visual edges of things intensifying and he laughed again. The man introduced himself with a name that Wade promptly forgot and then Wade told him his name and said that he was tripping, to explain away any behavior the man might consider odd. The sky was full of stars out here, although he could still see the darkness hovering over the harbor below.

The man said it was too bad about the show, he was really looking forward to it. He worked for a record company. It seemed just a little too weird the way it was stormy right down there and the wind was blowing and up here it was perfectly calm. The car pulled into a driveway that turned in a half circle between hedges. There were no visible neighbors and the lights of the city stretched out below. Oh, said Wade. The man took him inside.

A HALLWAY WITH WOOD FLOORS TURNED INTO A SUNKEN LIVING
room with sliding doors of glass that looked onto darkness with more
of a city view and a vaster darkness out there which was the ocean. A
woman was sprawled on the sofa, leafing through a magazine. She was
blonde and weathered and her feet and her hands were large. The man
was asking him about the band they had been planning to see, if he
really liked them, what he thought of their music; he was thinking of
signing them to his company's label. Wade explained that he was only
there to see the opening act.

Really, said the man. What are they like?

Wade searched for the appropriate words. They eluded him.

It's like uh . . . , he said finally.

Fucking death, he finished.

The man considered this.

You're using fucking as an adjective or a verb? he asked.

Wade pictured a diagram of words but got lost, as if achieving that
mental image of a structure of language was the point, the place he's
gotten to but now he can't get back to whatever they were talking
about.

Erotic, said the man. And dark?

Definitely, said Wade.

It was all an incredibly complex grid mixed up with that dead girl
and the way the life force exited. We need a new rule, the woman on
the couch was saying to the man. Only drug dealers and whores get to
have cellphones.

You're a big boy, said the woman to Wade, putting her magazine
down.

She seemed to be organically entwined with the sofa, symbiotically
enmeshed, in fact, something luxurious, expensive, rooted, and poison.

I'll have to investigate this band, said the man.

The woman offered Wade a truffle from a crystal bowl. It was the
most chocolate, ever.

Please, she said. Sit down. Have a drink or whatever.

She materialized a silver tray from somewhere without stepping
off of the sofa, pills and powders and buds arranged like confections.
Wade just shook his head. She opened up a capsule and dumped the

powder from inside into a fizzy drink.

The boy's tripping, said the man.

Well, she said. Then I imagine we'll be plenty of mental stimulation for him.

She handed him the fizzy drink. He was so thirsty. When it was all gone, he smelled powder, and remembered that pill.

What was in that drink? he asked.

It'll complexify things, said the woman.

She swallowed a pill of her own.

What was it, a roofie? he asked.

She laughed.

What, you afraid of a little date rape?

Wade kept thinking: bleary. Bleary, bleary, bleary. Finally, he thought. A crime.

THEY'RE NOT THE MOST INTERESTING NEW BODY PARTS, THE MAN said to the woman. She knew just what he meant.

Call Jerry, she said. Jerry gets to have a cellphone.

That's so literal of you, said the man. But then, you made the rule. He got on the phone.

Perhaps he'd like to hear that band you like so much, said the man.

Right, she said. Erotic and dark.

She stood and walked to the stereo. She was enormous. Wade wondered if she was as big as he was. It took her forever to do whatever was happening and Wade lost himself in various patterns of photographs and paintings which graced the wall. The abstract ones kept him busy enough, but the figurative ones were just too lively. His chair was leather and perfect. It was the most comfortable chair in all the world. The man mumbled and laughed into the phone and hung it up. It rang. The man spoke to someone in a foreign language and Wade began to think there was something really wrong here. The man said to the woman, He wants to know if foxes and bears get along. Do foxes and bears get along?

She thought about this.

They aren't predators or prey of each other, she said.

The man spoke again in the other language. Wade couldn't understand a word, but felt he was discussing the relative intelligence of a predator and its prey. As the man hung up the phone, the music began.

I'm afraid I have to go out, said the man. But there should be plenty here to keep you occupied.

He winked at Wade, which seemed to imply sex with the woman, and then he said some other things, and it sounded like he called the woman Sophie, but Wade wondered if he was confusing her with the furniture she had been so involved with. Is Jerry coming over? she asked.

The man left. The woman was back on the sofa with her eyes closed as if truly appreciating the music, which was barely audible, although it did seem now to be slowly growing and encroaching on his mind. Actually, it was getting truly ominous as if insinuating itself into the situation that everyone knew was going to get bad.

BY THE TIME THE MUSIC ENDED HE WAS EXHAUSTED. HE'D BEEN many places in that time but was too mentally overwhelmed to revisit or understand any of them. They sat for a moment in silence. Sophie opened her eyes.

You like it? she said.

He nodded. Her hair glistened in the room's dim lighting as if she'd placed lights inside of it.

Where are you from? he asked.

She laughed, as if at him, made a dismissive gesture.

It doesn't matter, she said. Probably the same place as you. We're all from the same place, aren't we? More or less?

Her face made Wade think that a map had come to life: a map of a dark and crowded state veined with roads that went nowhere and alleys where every human action was a financial transaction. The doorbell rang and a skinny gay man in shorts and a winged hat, what looked like a green felt shirt, was chattering in the living room. Karen, he kept saying Karen, but Wade couldn't imagine who Karen might be.

I'm almost out of Brain Eraser, he told her. Some of my clients, they're real weed hogs, want to buy up all the Brain Eraser. Look, I tell them, first things first. Med-i-cine.

Sophie was just fluttering and laughing. Suddenly, Wade wondered if he'd been infected. He had this thing on his forehead, too big to be a normal pimple. He was now certain he had AIDS; he thought of a few men it could have come from. But he had to forget it or he'd have a bad experience. He'd deal with AIDS tomorrow when he wasn't on drugs. Then he wasn't sure he'd be normal tomorrow, or that tomorrow would ever arrive. He tried to focus on Jerry's words. Jerry had grown up on a farm in Indiana. All the farmers back there were developing cancers, because of the chemicals. By the way, how's your slave? Jerry asked Sophie.

Succulent, said Sophie.

I need to be around sane people sometimes, Jerry said. Keep my context. This one girl, she thinks the president and everyone is really space aliens. She thinks it's just masks.

Sane people, said Sophie. Like me?

They cracked up, and then he was talking about some clients who heard voices. I know what that's about, said Jerry. I remember I was a kid at camp and this counselor came to my bed? A real cute one. I had two voices in my head then.

A figurative painting demanded Wade's attention. It was covered with magic lesions. This abstract man was unraveling and complexifying spirit and disease of flesh.

One voice is going No No No, Jerry was saying. The other one's going Yes Yes Yes.

Wade forced himself to stop staring at the painting. What is the issue here, thought Wade.

The Yes voice won that one, Jerry said, and the other voice went away for good.

Jerry's cellphone rang. He told whoever it was that he'd be in that neighborhood in about half an hour, and then he left.

The silence that remained was terrifying. Sophie looked at Wade with disappointment and sighed, settled back into her couch.

Did you grow up on a farm? he asked.

She sneered at him.

Look, she said. Maybe you're in over your head here.

Wade was sure there was an issue here, but then the word *issue* seemed ridiculous.

Maybe you should check out the primitive scene in the library, she said. It'll speak to your drugged and open mind.

He opened his mouth as if to speak. Her impatient hostility was like a palpable acid in the air scorching the tender membranes of his brain.

You know nothing about me, he said finally.

She just stared at him.

He brought me here, he said. I didn't ask to come. Your husband or whoever.

Husband? she said.

She laughed, wickedly, as he'd only seen before in cartoons.

You think I don't like you, she said. And that must make you very sad. Look at you. You think vanity is a sin. Probably you think games are wrong and you think the consolations of the rich are the root source of human misery. But you haven't lived.

She leaned back into the sofa, lit a cigarette.

You get tired of being street theater, she said. I'm not owned here.
There are certain agreements in place, contracts have been signed.

She waved her hand at the surroundings, then stood and began
enormously pacing.

They're designing babies, she said. But none like *me*. Broke the
mold on that one. What kind of babies you figure they want? Worker
babies. Drones. You suppose if they could have shown a spotlight
on the message from our genes—mine and yours I mean, mine and
yours—you think either one of us would still be here?

It's like Bronzi told me, she said. We don't *work*.

She laughed at her private joke.

Not that I think nature is some holy thing, she said. Nature never
did *me* any favors.

Her words required all of Wade's concentration. He didn't know
what nature meant. Was it a place, a force, an atmosphere, a filter?

Just fuck everything up, she said. Just make more profound monsters and deformities. Unleash the zoo.

Wade thought: *her hands are too big*. He thought they must belong to
somebody else. Somebody who maybe also had "ideas about the future."

Back in my youth, the woman said, way back then, I remember.
Bronzi DiMarco always carried a tiny pistol in her purse. I learned so
much from Miss Bronzi. She shot somebody once, and then we went
shopping. We just bought and bought. I've never felt so alive, it was
the most profound day of my girlhood. The future was irrelevant, only
the present. Let it *all* happen, I thought. Live in the *now*. I had met
Bronzi some time before that at the welfare office. Doing my paperwork
under the ghastly fluorescent lights. I had my little mess of pride, you
know, I thought gosh, I don't want my caseworker think I'm lazy. I
don't want her to think I *never* had a job. Oh no, Bronzi said. You just
write zero on every line. You say, I *don't* work.

Sophie picked up a newspaper. Wade felt that women he met were
always doing this.

Oh, looky here, she said. A former exotic dancer was acquitted of
involuntary manslaughter, but found guilty on drug-use charges. Her
van ran off the freeway outside of Vegas and killed six teenagers who
were picking up litter. That's an awful lot in one fell swoop, wouldn't

you say?

Wade couldn't tell if she was joking, so his mouth twisted into something halfway a smile of appreciation and halfway a confused grimace. The newspaper was a noisy cloud or magic screen. It was Sophie's attitude towards its so-called tragedies that seemed instructive. Sophie told him about the Filipina who was the latest president of her country. At a press conference, she'd been questioned about rumors of a coup by a particular general. Oh, I don't think so, she said. In front of everyone, she rang up the general on her cellphone. Are you planning a coup against me? she asked.

That's what they're for, said Sophie, as if it proved a point she'd been making. Drug dealers, whores, and fabulous Filipinas, she said. Those are the only ones who get cellphones.

It seemed she was a big fan of Filipinas. She quoted Imelda Marcos. *They thought they'd find skeletons in my closet, but fortunately all they found was shoes—beautiful shoes.* Sophie found this hilarious. Wade wondered if there was something inherently funny about monstrous, stylish women that he'd never before appreciated.

But now she was saddened, theatrically. She wasn't a fan of police states after all. One of her friends, Miss Cootie Dentata, had been beaten by the police in Manila. They hate glamour and beauty as much as Americans do, she said, and she turned away dramatically to either hide her emotions or call attention to their grandeur. She composed herself, addressed one of the paintings, the painting with AIDS.

You look at the world and you think we're being punished, she said. But what if that wasn't the case at all. What if this was enchantment. I just don't want to be disenchanted, she said. But I think it was just a phase, I think it's ending now. You can't be bored, you have to make it always new, always more complicated.

She turned and faced him abruptly.

How are the visuals? she asked.

Wade nodded.

Really good, he said.

Here, she said, and she towered over him with a book of cartoons.

Excuse me, she said next, and she left the room.

WAS SHE WEEPING? SOMEWHERE IN THE DISTANCE, IN THE HOUSE; he was sure of it.

HE COULDN'T FOLLOW THE WORDS IN THE BUBBLES, BUT THE images were exploding, actually now inside his brain. Outrageously muscled men and humanoid creatures were often gagged and bound and monsters with human bodies but lizard heads or quasi-canine heads or black globes with red eyeslits for heads were strutting through netherworlds and tunnel worlds and silvery metallic worlds with enormous scaly or chrome or knobbed erections. Here was a surreally handsome blue-eyed youth, the features of a twelve-year-old but the exaggerated muscley physique of a World Federation wrestler, laid belly down on a car hood, wrists tied to windshield wipers, ankles bound, rump plumped up, neck twisted looking back in innocent terror and expectation.

It's a mystery, Sophie said. She had snuck back in without his noticing, and was standing somewhere behind him. The word "mystery" seemed to detach, to float and collide with more sensual concepts.

There's a lot of holes in the plot, she continued. There's been a crime, but you aren't sure what.

He glanced down at the open comic book in his lap. A boy and a girl who looked like twins were tied up in a closet. The story was disintegrating into shards of color, nonsense that did or didn't form a pattern. He looked away.

He looked back to see if any of the panels resembled memories. The boy's ass was in need of a good spanking. Wade felt like *Wade* was about to be punished, but that the word "spanking" had grown out of control, was threatening the very fabric of space and time. Senators were present and a number of men in capes, a black hole. Travel through space in order *to be observed and studied.*

The obvious possibility, Sophie said, is that victim, victimizer, and detective all turn out to be the same person. A simple case of multiple personality. As the detective, you don't want to explore that possibility. You know, I used to hold certain beliefs. But I don't believe in those things anymore.

She walked away, voice trailing off, Entities and what-have-you . . .

HE TURNED THE PAGE. FOCUSED ON WORDS IN THE BUBBLES OF speech, flipping faster to jumble them into a more condensed narrative.

who call them black holes—black because they cannot emit light holes yield unto the angels' vampire games, and it wasn't long before I felt his lips on a wounded boy, so I'd give him an examination. bottomless with a foundation of light. And establish the solar system-like atomic model with which most of us are a ripple results in what we commonly refer to as gravity. Desire for a boy is noxious dew, and smoke. Doors of fire separate these They Should he ever see have come on her behalf, and pray to the exhausting possibilities each of these theories—they differ only in the final details. I went to her but soon the time began to drag. I wasn't used to living cause she insisted on enjoying full Let's consider in more detail the perspective of an observer on nine inches long crooked & curved Daddy's in control shall pursue to destroy the enemy in the fuck me in several different positions . . .

IT WAS CLEAR TO WADE THAT THE NORMAL PRACTICE OF LANguage was an unacceptable sort of prison. She was suggesting that, with her outrageous use of words. Her words were like probes, experimenting with shapes and possibilities. If some of those words were evil, well, that was a random evolutionary byproduct. He waited a moment, then looked around. Shut the comic book. He needed to leave. He could see the city spread out below and the air would be so cool and dark out there and he could walk through it hidden and alive. He felt hot and flushed and like he was vibrating to the point he'd destroy something crystalline if he didn't soon escape.

Hello? he said. He had to tell her he was leaving, he couldn't just disappear.

The hallway was unnaturally long and too short.

Hello? he said.

He found the room with the primitive scenes, art from Africa with superpronated postures and white slits for eyes, astonished or scary expressions and he realized that the expressions were an act: they were contrived, and this was funny.

Hello? he said, back in the hallway, and he felt easier now, for it was clear that just as these scary totems were a mask over benevolence, well, it was the same thing with her.

Hello? he said.

He entered the room cautiously, as if it could shatter. The room just sat there and then it stopped being the room; it broke down into bed, carpet, mirror, closet. Plush carpet. He had to take off his shoes and walk on the carpet. The closet door was wide open and he caught a glimpse. He told himself he'd look in just one second, but right now he was concentrating on the carpet between his toes.

A SKI MASK HUNG ON A PEG. IT WAS LIKE A FAMILIAR FACE IN the closet. He tried on a furry jacket instead, found a wad of money in the pocket. The money wasn't green. Or else the green of the money was interwoven with blue sparks of electricity, which sometimes predominated, and with the brown of excrement. The faces were those of the usual dead presidents, but something was off, their eyes were asymmetrical and gazed in slightly different directions. Sometimes they weren't dead presidents at all, but the sadistic demons who ruled and were worshipped in America. Or else the intricate multilayered printing on the bills was the maze of death which hid the presence of fluctuating and luminous and divinely empathetic beings. The theft of the magic money was a crime that Wade knew to be completely irrelevant, a distraction from truly meaningful actions which probably were also crimes, but in a less technical sense. He stood in front of the full-length mirror holding the ski mask. It was as if he was standing there holding his own face and so he put it on. And it was his own face.

Somebody groaned and Wade wondered if it was himself groaning. He zipped up his pants. He crossed the hallway to another bedroom, which was empty. But something was alive in the closet.

The ski mask gave him courage. He was both terrifying and terrified. The ceiling of the room was arched and creamy and imprinted with designs that Wade couldn't make out. It's called relief, he remembered, and it's faces. The word "relief" was funny, but he stopped himself from smiling. The gold trim went around and around and around. He'd been looking at it for too long.

THIS PERSON WAS LIKE AN ANCIENT IMAGE OF SUFFERING IN-scribed in Wade's spinal column or lung. There was something so twisted about the musculature. Wade was afraid he'd receive an electric shock if he touched him. That didn't make sense, but he was paralyzed.

I'll be right back, he said. The mouth was duct-taped shut. Wade thought to rip the tape off, but worried there'd be a scream.

He made his way down the hall to the sunken living room. She wasn't there, but the phone was on the mantle.

The dial tone contained too many possibilities.

I'm too fucked up, he thought. What sort of criminal network of abduction and snuff films he'd wandered into and what they might do with him. There were far more banal possibilities, of course. That guy's terror had seemed staged. The world of sirens and uniforms and crackling intercoms would be a nightmare of regular pain. He sat in the comfortable chair to gather his wits.

The ropes made the ass seem so . . . primordial. Separate and hungry. All of his thoughts were just the prison of language. The thought of fucking the ass floored him. He looked through CDs as if song titles might tell him what to do. This at least reminded him that there were other possibilities besides doing it to the captive "prison style" or calling the cops. He wondered where he'd heard that phrase, "prison style."

THE SKY OUTSIDE WAS FULL OF STARS. HE REMEMBERED MUSIC he'd heard and it was the saddest music. He felt that people were moving around in the dark, and in the house, but he didn't feel like he was being watched. He felt like he should be being watched. No, that wasn't it. He felt like he was two different people, one watching the other. He was curious to see what he would do next.

Walked slowly back to the bedroom. The closet was empty, and he wondered if he was in the right room, pictured an endless maze of identical bedrooms along ominous hallways, he'd never find his way. The next bedroom was dark, a video was playing on the television, but nobody was there. Old, in black and white, it seemed like a transmission from a dead generation.

HE WAS HURTLING NOW THROUGH THE SCRUB ON THE DARK hillside with too much momentum. Stopped his descent, sliding in the dust and gasping for breath. He could never breathe enough of the cool outside air. There was wind. Wind. He'd left his jacket behind. Stopped for a moment, then continued down at a sideways angle to keep gravity from propelling him too fast. He imagined for a moment he was in a different life altogether. That helicopters would shine lights on the dark hills searching for him, a wanted man. He had been living in the crevices and canyons, capturing garter snakes and cooking them over small fires.

It wasn't storming anymore, anywhere. As his eyes became accustomed to the dark, he looked down at himself to see a stain on the front of his shirt, moist and reddish like blood. He still had the ski mask in his left hand.

Report #4

[The following Report is signed "Mike A." and is a
follow-up report on the call concerning the "muddy,
bloody, mumbling white man" who had been reported in
the ladies restroom by Manager Joseph K. the night
before. No investigation was made the night before
by officer Regina M., and this follow-up report was
not made until 9 P.M. on Oct. 6th, 24 hours after
the initial report. The blood scrapings that were
later "lost" by Detective R. are not detailed in this
report.]
WEST CITY POLICE DEPARTMENT CRIMINAL INVESTIGATION
FIELD REPORT
TYPE OF OFFENSE: General Information
LOCATION OF OFFENSE: B.
VICTIM(S):
DATE OCCURRED: 10-5
[this date seems to be referring to the date of the
original call as opposed to the date when this report
was made]
TIME OCCURRED: 9:00 - 9:30 P.M.
NUMBER OF SUSPECTS IN CUSTODY:
IS THERE EVIDENCE STORED IN EVIDENCE VAULT:

PG 1 OF 2
SUMMARY OF INVESTIGATION
10/6 Received call to go to Chucky Cheese's + talk to
the Manager.
10/6 9:00 P.M. Det. Sgt. A. + Det. R. went to Chucky
Cheese + talked with the manager, a Joseph K. [Mr. K's
address and phone number is listed here and highlighted
along with his name]. Joseph K related that they had a
White / male on 10/5 Between 9:00 - 9:30 AM [the "AM"
seems to contradict all other reports and is probably
an error] that a White / male was Found the ladies
bathroom bleeding from the arm. the Manager stated
that the white man was tall, maybe 6'5" Dirty, 20's,
Pair of Sunglasses were left in toilet suspected by
White / male. the White male Appeared to be Mental / +
Disorentated (Possible intoxicated or under inFluence

of Drugs) Police were called Subject left out on Foot +
Walked East toward the back Dumpster then [additional
text is inserted here at the bottom of the page in the
report] White males Clothing was blue T-shirt, Black
shoes, look like tennis shoes. Black thin warm up
pants.
PAGE 2 OF 2
Came back out to San Jacinto + walked toward Chevron
Service Station.
10/6 9:00 P.M. Det. Sgt. A. + Det. R. Det. R. took
blood scrapings from North Wall inside women's bathroom
above toilet, took blood scrapings From inside OF door
to women's bathroom + Entrance hall to bathroom From
Sitting Area at Chucky Cheese.
SIGNATURE OF INVESTIGATING OFFICER: [signed] Mike A.

From Medical Examiner's Report (continued)

According to Dr. F., who had been the boy's doctor,
the abrasions on the boy's penis, which were likely
self-inflicted, were not necessarily related to this
particular episode. They do however, indicate a
sexualized child, which suggests a child who is being
sexually abused.

Report #7

Fiber expert, Chuck S. of the West Coast Institute of
Forensic Sciences disputed the "red fiber" (Evidence#
B4556) its microscopic similarity to the rayon crime-
scene fiber. Stated Chuck S, "Fiber evidence has taken
on considerable prestige in the public's mind in recent
years, but, professional law enforcement personnel are
not as impressed. The FBI now includes in all bureau
fiber evidence reports a standard disclaimer about
its inherent unreliability. Fibers are not comparable
to fingerprints--or dental imprints, for that matter.
In order for a probable match to have significance in
a case like this, it must be shown that the fibers
being tested have an exclusive source--as opposed to
so common a source that any match is meaningless. The
red rayon fiber--found not on Suspect's clothing but

on Suspect's lover's robe--is traceable to the type of material used to make most of the variety of jerseys for sale at the local Wal-Mart, which, by virtue of being the only large retail store in the area, was frequented by nearly every local resident."

THE MAN WAS FROM ITALY. WADE MET HIM IN THE VIDEO ARCADE
of the adult bookstore in town. Wade had exchanged one kind of
money for a new kind, gold coins with the names of different astro-
logical signs on them. When he put them in a slot, the video screen
came to life. Wade discovered that Italian words were kind of like the
Spanish words he'd studied in junior high. If Wade looked directly at
the Italian man, the man turned into a Picasso painting. This made him
compelling, but sometimes it got out of control and Wade had to look
away. The porn itself was less demanding. It wouldn't morph, but remained shoddy realist surface. The two of them groped for expressions
they could both understand. The words were a concrete presence, like
humidity between them. In this way, Wade discovered that language
was a bridge and an atmosphere. It seemed like an innovative way for
brains to create a shared space in and outside of themselves. He felt
like he remembered it as a technological advance. He got into the man's
car. The limitations of their language made the sheer animal warmth of
their shared presence more relaxing. The exhausting task of creating
concepts limited their desire to do anything but drive on toward the
north. It rained in the Central Valley and hundreds of trucks sprayed
them with their effluence so that it was like driving in and out of
car washes at incredible speeds. By the time they arrived, just after
dawn, the warmth of the man's apartment in San Francisco was like an
abstract sexual organ.

Sometime after, Wade slept. Woke and slept and slept.

Colorless.

THE ITALIAN FIXED WADE BREAKFAST. WADE ATE AND WENT
back to sleep. At some point this exact scenario repeated itself, so that
Wade felt he had been having repeated dreams of sitting at the table
in a red-striped velour bathrobe cradling a mug of coffee. The Italian
wanted to go hiking. He drove Wade out to Land's End, took him to
a spot where men were cruising in the bushes. Wade let him unzip
Wade's pants and go at it for a minute before he shoved the man away,
disappeared into the brush. In a clearing he came across a pudgy man
in a lawnchair, wearing only fishnet stockings and high-heeled shoes.
He was listening to his portable radio, and he smiled at Wade. Wade
admired his will. He felt that this man had succeeded at creating a
unique perspective. An inexpressible sensation relevant to matter, he
thought, but wasn't sure what this meant.

He cut onto a smaller trail. A stranger began mumbling to him and
fondling himself. Wade had no idea what he was saying, but liked the
idea that the Italian had brought him into the wilderness, but now he'd
leave with someone different. He was about to ask the stranger to drive
him somewhere, when he saw a teenager watching him through the
bushes. Wade sauntered over, asked the kid what was going on. The
kid said he was looking to hang out with a nice person. Wade thought
that if you believed something about yourself it might become true.
I'm a cruel man, a man who doesn't care. The kid wasn't exactly handsome, but his awkwardness was charming. Wade asked him if he'd ever
done anything before; the kid said he liked to do everything. When I
was a boy, Wade said, I met this teenager. He had me touch his dick.

Wade was surprised that the boy didn't excite him. What he
felt instead was a certain "tenderness." Wade stuck his hand under
the waistband of the kid's jogging pants and touched the boy's ass.
Because the Italian had saved him, his betrayal was exhilarating. He
remembered what that woman had said about shooting people, and
then shopping.

He showed me how to tie certain knots he'd learned in Cub Scouts,
said Wade. I asked him to demonstrate. I asked him to explain sex to
me and show me what a rape was. He was twelve.

Twelve isn't a teenager, said the kid.

This disturbed Wade, and momentarily confused him.

I'm eighteen, the kid said.

You have ID? asked Wade. He moved his hand around the front and jacked the kid off. He was pleased that he could turn this "tenderness" into arousal. The kid fumbled in his pocket, as if he thought Wade would actually stop touching him if he couldn't document his obvious lie. Wade wondered why he'd told him that story, as if all sex involving teenagers was fundamentally the same. The kid flashed his school ID. I have some regulars, said the boy, but one of them is gone now. Wade didn't know what he was talking about. He led him up the path, into the trees.

WE'RE IN THE SIXTH GREAT DIE-OFF, THE BOY TOLD HIM.

Apparently he could think of nothing else to say. In the history of the earth, this die-off ranked third so far. He'd learned that fact at school.

YOU LIKE IT GENTLE OR YOU LIKE IT ROUGH? ASKED WADE. THE boy looked at him like he didn't understand.

OH, SHIT, SAID THE BOY. OW.

You want me to stop? asked Wade.

The boy looked panicked.

No, he said. I just need to relax. If you just keep doing it, I'll start to relax.

Ow, he said. Fuck.

Hold still, said Wade. I'll get it back in. What's that? Are you okay?

It's nothing, said the boy. I said if you just keep doing it.

AFTERWARD, WADE HAD TO FIGHT HIS IMPULSE TO GIVE THE BOY something. Instead, the boy gave *him* a piece of paper, with his pager number on it. Wade decided the boy was spoiled, but wasn't sure if that had made it more pleasurable or less.

Later, Wade began to think of that house on the hill as "the scene of the crime." On the other hand, his skills of interpretation had been scrambled. He tried to compose the body in his mind. Underarm hair? He couldn't remember.

He knew he'd be compelled to return there someday. But not yet. He called the number on the paper, thinking that the boy's naked body would give him a point of reference, but the number was temporarily out of service, and would remain so forever. He found himself instead wandering into another endless western summer: the units on vacation and the freeways and the mining town museums. *The distinctive mountain which dominates the skyline is a basalt-capped mesa of volcanic origin. Proof of the community's fondness for its most recognizable landscape can be found in the countless times its image has been captured by local artists and used in the logos and names of local businesses.* Cheap motels full of family, a teenage boy with a Jimi Hendrix T-shirt, and a baby girl stumbling across the parking lot. Dead animals, archaic ranching implements, and wagon wheels decorated everything, and pine trees drooped into the sun. Ten minutes after checkout time, last oversized vehicle in the parking lot, the teenage boy yelled *Shut up* to somebody, and the birds fell silent.

That woman had taught him that the world was a cheap facade. Pleasure, then, was to be found in simultaneously erecting outrageous surfaces and picking them apart to reveal the bullshit underneath. It wasn't hard to be welcomed as a player into the games for the pettiest stakes imaginable. It wasn't as if the players only lost. They won and they won and they won.

At six o'clock in the afternoon in the middle of July the daylight seared the rearview mirrors and the automobiles and the business suits at service stations outside desert cities and there was no room left in any heart as far as the eye could see no opening no breath only the sound of a car door slamming shut. The dark side of the American Dream, somebody said to him once, and he woke for a moment from his heartbreak and said to them Side? Side? What do you mean side? There's only one side here. Where is the other? How do you get there? He kept on like this until he was speaking only to himself. He sat on a curb at seven o'clock in the July afternoon and tried to form his body into a hole he could burrow into.

That house back there was what he had come to think of as society, a term he sometimes confused with civilization. It wasn't that the world he lived in now was somehow not those things. He was aware that he was using words in that old way that was "like" a prison; in the same way that society was "like" a prison. He was bored with thinking about how words worked. It didn't really matter. There had been a crime, and everything was constructed around that. It had all been alluded to in that comic book. Buildings and people and laws repulsed him. The aggression of sprinkler systems.

He wasn't sure now what kind of life he'd been tricked into living. All around him, the people looked tricked. He didn't know what it was he might want instead. He guessed he was reaching that point where he'd start to think, I'm not a young man anymore. He wanted to live in a transformed world, pregnant with magic. He would learn not to be entranced by the trivia. Which was practically everything. Or was everything, in which case the opposite path was equally valid.

He felt that the time had come to make some sort of decision. Develop a strategy, and change his habits. He began reading flyers stapled to telephone poles and billboards. The options involved getting in touch with his spiritual side, raising money for environmental causes, or acquiring computer skills. When he thought about filling out a job application, it frightened him; he was sure he'd end up killing people. He wanted to walk into the nearest building and ask for work as a rapist. That's what I do, he would say. I rape.

I practice victimless rape, he told the imaginary interviewer. I rape without an object. I just am raping, all the time . . .

He realized that he was not only babbling, but babbling out loud. This reinforced the idea that he had to "change his path." He decided he'd acquire computer skills. He would navigate the web. This web was trying to sever itself altogether from society, he thought. Wasn't that worth a try? Promises were being made that nobody intended on keeping. He would speak the language of machines. He drew a picture of a robot, then ripped it into pieces. He gave each different piece a name. Finally, he named himself: Wade, he said, is short for Wild Game.

HE CAME TO AN EXPANSE OF SALT, AND THE CITY THAT ACCOM-
panied it. A phrase came to him in this city: *the firstborn of the dead.*
Everything was in its proper place here, and that wasn't working. Of
all the cheap hotels he could seek refuge in, he found it in the cheapest.
The acrid smell of the carpets and the stained mattress were evidence
that other humans had at least passed through this way. In theory, at
least, he wasn't the only one.

HE WAS DOZING ON A BUS. HE'D TAKEN A TRIP ACROSS THE COUN-
try, and now he was returning west. The motivation for this trip had
been another brief affair. Bewilderment and terror, the man had said
to Wade, criticizing Wade's manner. Wade didn't see the issue. All of
his most intimate pleasures seemed tied to "bewilderment and terror."
You mustn't mistake the art form of my persona for hostility either, his
lover had said, finally. It was time for Wade to go.

It wasn't a bus that carried him along dozing, but a plane. This
could mean that Wade had become a different sort of person. But people flew all the time, it wasn't unusual; the steward was urging him to
solve a case. Wade wasn't sure if he was chosen because he was really
a detective, or only because everyone else on board was asleep. The
steward asked him to choose between the ravioli and the chicken. He
was surprised that the plane hadn't crashed yet. They'd been delayed
on the runway because of some difficulty between the engine and its
oxygen supply.

The steward adored certain passengers, a "pop group feminina." He
urged them to sing, and they did, in unison, just as they'd answered
his questions. Airplane crashes were one of society's favorite ways of
giving its citizens bewilderment and terror. Wade tried to sleep again;
ferns in the silvery mist. Police would be mystified by the coroner's
discovery that, at the time of the crash, one of the passengers was
already dead.

HE LIKED TO REMIND HIMSELF THAT HE WASN'T A RELIABLE WIT-
ness. He'd been looking for some sort of climax, and so he'd mistaken
the banality of human sex acts for crime. The banality of fulfillable
desire. Unless that's what crime was. He'd been drugged, and so was
equally a victim. It wasn't his essential self that was revealed, just a
meaningless accident of chemistry. He decided that nobody really
wanted to be saved.

The city he'd just come from had been an architectural nightmare.
The legendary sadness of its inhabitants was just the natural human
relationship to such a vast jailhouse by the sea.

Nobody else had ever spoken to him like that woman. She was the
most essentially cynical, masculine person he'd ever met. It was necessary, then, that she had been weeping. He needed to believe that she
was heartbroken and complete. Hadn't he discovered something? That
it was all living? And that certain constructs or masks could stand
in for living, replace its scarier parts. She was really a sweetheart.
"Really" wasn't what he meant exactly; it wasn't a true sweetness hiding behind a false facade. It was more like hell was a place that was
always going on. Once you accepted that, other things could happen.
Those passengers were now singing a love song, which involved proud
references to the flag of their territory, an American colony of sorts,
that wasn't exactly independent and wasn't exactly owned.

IN SAN FRANCISCO, HE RETURNED TO THE CRUISY BUSHES NEAR Land's End. He was surprised to run into the Italian there. It was as if all the intervening time had been negated, some mirage or trance state, and his real life had always been back here with the shrubs, cruising and picking up men. Remembering how much he'd enjoyed abandoning him the first time, he went home with the Italian. The Italian had been taking English lessons and was eager to reduce the mystery.

While Wade was fucking him from the front, he put his hands around the man's throat and gently choked him, at the same time that he kissed him.

Why do you know how to love me? the Italian said afterward. Wade napped. The next day, he was again sitting around in a red-striped velour robe. Wade insisted they go back out to the trees. The Italian was terrified. Promise me, he said. Wade knew the man liked to have sex in the dirt too much to resist. He promised.

Instead of Land's End, the Italian took Wade to Fairy Lane, between the windmills at the edge of Golden Gate Park. Signs warned men to keep on the paths, for the sake of the vegetation. Wade shoved the Italian into the dirt; he licked Wade's black tennis shoes. Wade pulled down the man's pants, and slapped his ass. No, not here, said the Italian, which was exactly the opposite of what he meant.

What was a word? A fleeting vibration. A firework.

I'll be right back, Wade said.

Off to one side, through the trees was a soccer field. The most electric, yellowy, froggy green. A chain-link fence had recently been built around it.

The field was empty. Wade found himself speaking with a dapper salt-and-pepper type. This man was in his fifties, but looked like he could have been thirty-nine. He was a big fan of public sex. Who wants to go *home* with somebody? asked the man. Into their pathetic little holes?

The Italian was chatting amiably with an older man in tan slacks. Tan slacks, tan slacks. This was how Wade would always think about this man, the man in the tan slacks. He wondered how the Italian could be speaking so energetically in his crappy broken English. The salt-and-pepper man sat on a stump, motioned for Wade to join him.

Used to be full of men here, he said. Guess they're all on the internet now.

Wade had never acquired those computer skills. The idea that gay men all over the world were sitting in chairs and looking at screens made the atmosphere here lush, intense, and sad. The sadness of everything that was passing away.

They've completely deforested it, the man told Wade. Used to be so thick with trees you'd never know the Great Highway was on one side and the soccer field on the other.

188 • STEPHEN BEACHY

EVERYTHING WAS PASSING AWAY. THE FILTERED LIGHT AND THE smell of eucalyptus and the animal bodies and the sadness itself. Such lonely blue butterflies fluttering toward death. Such delicate blue flowers. They are blue, sky blue, very blue. They are like reeds in the wind; the ones which glisten, which bend.

Flowers are the misery I create, thought Wade. He'd heard that line somewhere; it was from a culture now extinct. He imagined some fascist, busybody groundskeeper clearing the world until there were no more places to hide. What would be left wouldn't be worth redecorating. He consoled himself: you couldn't really create a smooth space. Space would always bend and wrinkle to accommodate us. Wade wasn't sure who he meant exactly by "us." Despite that confusion, he concluded this line of thinking: *we will bend it and wrinkle it ourselves.*

HE WALKED. A FEW MEN FOLLOWED HIM. HE TOOK A FORK IN THE path and almost walked into Tan Slacks.

Tan Slacks talked about such banal things that Wade couldn't focus on meaning. Tan Slacks dealt in rocks. He always said "stones" or "gems," but every time he said "stones" or "gems," Wade said to himself "rocks." He couldn't help it. After they had sex in the man's East Bay apartment, overlooking a shallow lake, the man received a phone call.

Ricky's not going to hire someone to kill you, Wade heard the man say. He just likes to think of himself as the sort of person who could do that if he wanted.

TAN SLACKS INVITED WADE TO COME ALONG FOR A "SOCIAL visit." In the car he told Wade about these people, Ricky and Dhoji, who he'd done so many good deeds for. He'd given Ricky the money to bring his wife to America in the first place, but last year when he took Ricky to a gem show in Arizona, Dhoji moved out with the kids. *Rock show*, thought Wade.

Dhoji lived in Oakland near the MacArthur BART. The apartment was on the ground floor, in the front of the building, and young men on tiny bikes were just outside the window. Inside, it was steaming; the thermostat had two settings, ninety degrees and off. Dhoji called the rock guy Brad to his face, but every time he stepped outside to smoke, she referred to him as "Ricky's sugar daddy." The children were two and three, a quiet boy with curly locks and painted toenails, and a precocious girl who chattered away. The rock guy referred to them several times as Irish twins, which amused him to no end. He clearly wanted Wade to ask him what an Irish twin was, but Wade wouldn't do it. Daddy says he's going to kill Mommy, said the little girl. Dhoji was in a state.

So I go over to Ricky's house for Jamyang's birthday party, she said. And Ricky says he's going to keep the kids and I never going to see them again. He says I am unfit mother.

Oh, Dhoji, he's not going to do any such thing, said the man. Did you have another fight?

His mother is there from Arizona, said Dhoji, and she gives me this present, this cosmetics? She is beautician, total trash woman. She gives me this face cream, I open it up, already has big handprint in it. No, really. Totally dug out. She just stick her hand in, take it all up. I call her American white trash.

The boy was wearing a Batman cape and now sucking on the skinny plastic tits of a mermaid Barbie, and the girl was playing with some food she didn't like. Dhoji tried to feed her a banana and the girl kept saying, *Aga.*

That is Tibetan for disgusting, Dhoji explained to Wade.

But he brought you back the kids, said the rock guy.

Of course he did, said Dhoji. He don't really want them, he has to go to work. But so I am like, okay, you keep the kids, we will see. I set up job for this Tibetan woman in Emeryville? Four days work, ten dollars an hour. But then Ricky come, he leave the kids out front of the house. He just leave them outside. You think I can call the police?

The telephone rang and Dhoji spoke into it in Hindi or Tibetan while rushing in and out of the kitchen, where curried potatoes, and okra with chili, and lentils were cooking. The rock guy went out to the front step of the building to smoke. Dhoji hung up and turned to Wade.

You know how to shoot person up with needle? she asked.

Wade just gazed at her.

Ricky's sugar daddy not gonna be able to do it, she said. I know that.

Her expression suggested that Ricky's sugar daddy disgusted her in some fundamental way. He came back in.

So when did he threaten to kill you? he asked.

I take kids to his office, said Dhoji. I going to drop them there, in his office. He tells me he's going to kill me. In front of other people I say, okay, is that real, you going to kill me or what, Ricky? He makes nice face and just says, Oh no, Dhoji, you're my children's mother, I love you, I could never hurt you, but then he come up and whisper in my ear. He says watch your back. He says he going to hire somebody to do it. He says they not even going to be able to recognize my face.

The sugar daddy sighed and shook his head, as if Ricky was a naughty child. Dhoji's kids were shoving chocolates into their faces.

They are total American trash kids, Dhoji said. Sugar and Power Rangers and Burger King.

The children weren't shy with Wade. They liked to be twirled, bounced, flown.

You like kids, Dhoji said.

No, said Wade. Not at all. But I like these two okay.

They seemed cynical for toddlers and androgynous, and they didn't much whine. They watched hyperactive cartoons that reminded him of the comic he'd read "back there." The outfits were less revealing, the bondage scenes less overt.

You wanna go to Las Vegas? Dhoji was asking. Lamont wanna go to Las Vegas, his gramma's having her eighty-year birthday. Next week we all gonna go.

The sugar daddy told Dhoji that if she kept inviting strange men to live with her, her children were going to get molested.

You think so? Dhoji said. Or you just don't like black guys.

That Tibetan army guy was the worst, said the sugar daddy.

Dhoji conceded that this was true. He had been smoking crack all night, and feeling harassed by the boys out front on their tiny bikes. He ran out with kitchen knives in each hand. There was also a Bhutanese guy, and a white eighteen-year-old who was obsessed with India and Buddhism, a roommate of Ricky's best friend. Dhoji referred to him as David Baldhead, to distinguish him from some other David.

He thinks India is la-la-la, said Dhoji. He been only three weeks in India his whole life, thinks he know everything. I think he is gay, but he don't know it yet. I think I'll get a dildo, I'm gonna fuck David Baldhead in the ass.

She turned to Wade.

What you think? she said. You think I should fuck David Baldhead in the ass?

Wade looked around, as if she might be addressing somebody else.

Sure, if he wants you to. Why not?

But didn't you pick up Lamont at a bus stop? asked the sugar daddy.

That was *other* one, said Dhoji. I never bring him here my house. I meet Lamont at Laney College.

He's going to cosmetology school too? asked the sugar daddy.

No, he's not *going* to school, said Dhoji.

The sugar daddy went outside again to smoke another cigarette. You are kind of smartass, Dhoji said to Wade. Don't look like it, but I can see.

She smiled, and he thought smartasses were a category she enjoyed. He had no idea what this perception was based on, however. He wondered if she could sense that he'd been involved in a crime. He thought that Dhoji was someone who liked to shock people. A neighbor girl stopped in and said hello, and sat there for a minute gazing at the soap opera now on the television, and Dhoji told Wade and the girl how scared she was this time really of her baby-daddy. She recapped the story of Ricky's death threats. She told then of the time when she was still living with Ricky, they'd been fighting and she said she wished that he was dead. She wished he'd arrange for the children's financial future and then just go off and die. Ricky handed her a gun and told her to just go ahead and shoot him then, or shoot herself and get it over with. It was a big gun, and he put the barrel in his mouth and handed her the other end.

The sugar daddy came back in, and shook his head in a condescending sort of way.

Ricky doesn't have enough money to hire somebody to kill you, he told Dhoji.

No, but Ricky's mother, she has money, said Dhoji.

The neighbor girl left, but then Dhoji's ex-boyfriend, the eighteen-year-old David Baldhead, rapped on the front window. He had two of his friends along with him, and Wade saw the sugar daddy's face light up.

Wade often encountered this sort of person. This sort of person was always driving around in someone else's car. These cars were not properly registered or insured. They had ripped seats where the upholstery edged out, seat covers made of a dirty cream-colored sheep's mush. Most of these people weren't licensed to drive, yet drive they did. This particular car was Ricky's, a car he'd bought with a loan from the sugar daddy himself.

194 • STEPHEN BEACHY

I'LL HAVE A TALK WITH RICKY, THE SUGAR DADDY PROMISED
Dhoji. We'll come by and check on you tomorrow. We'll take the kids
out or something. Go to the park.

In the car, he confided to Wade that the gun Ricky had put in his
mouth and offered to Dhoji that day hadn't been loaded at all. He just
wanted to see if she would do it. He just wanted to make sure she
wasn't that crazy.

They love their dramas and their cruel little games, the sugar daddy
said. But there isn't really any death at the center. They want to think
it's a dangerous whirlwind, with death at the center, but it just isn't so.

Oh, it is too, thought Wade. He remembered the corpse of the girl
at that club. He was so tired of listening to this man talk. He imagined
for a moment that this was some movie he'd stepped into, in which
case he would surely kill Dhoji's husband for her, failing to perceive
some inevitable complication or secret alliance. A less knotted version
involved social service agencies and slogans about domestic abuse. The
possibility that there was some part for him to play here, some falseness
or irrelevance, depressed him. He didn't want to love any children or
care if the world was blackened and every living thing murdered until
only some robotic homogenized humans were left humming around
the globe.

Have you ever been to Vegas? the sugar daddy asked him.

No, he said. I never have.

THE NEXT DAY FOUND THEM AT A TRAILHEAD LEADING INTO THE East Bay hills. A cop car swooped through the parking lot. Peace *aga*, said the children, peace *aga*.

They learn that from Stephen Jonathan, said Dhoji. They are saying the police is *aga*.

A man named Ralph was with them, and David Baldhead, and a gay Moroccan man, Salah, who had lived as Ricky and Dhoji's roommate at some time in the past. He had kept their apartment spotlessly clean, as he hadn't paid any rent. His English was very proper, as if he'd acquired it in a completely different context from the one in which he was now immersed. The winter light was tepid, and the trail was moist. The sugar daddy was talking to Salah about his own trip to Morocco, and a place called the Djema el-Fnaa.

Oh, yes, Salah said. Quite an architectural wonder it is. The largest square in the world.

I'd heard so much about it, the sugar daddy was saying. The ancient storytellers and monkey-jugglers and drummers and the like.

The path had horse shit in it, and the children were saying *aga*. *Aga* was their favorite word. It delighted them to no end to declare various aspects of the world disgusting. Shit, food, police, cows, and other babies. The things they liked—Batman, Barbie, Wade, pink, purple, airplanes—paled in comparison to the pleasures of the disgusting.

An old man was pouring boiling water on his hands and asking for money, the sugar daddy was saying. He laughed.

Go ahead and scald your feet and I'll give you another dirham, I told him.

The little boy Jamyang was walking with his bottle, but tiring, and wanted Wade to carry him. They wandered off ahead of the group, and up a hillside where you could see Richmond and Berkeley stretched out below, and the Bay, San Francisco and the Marin headlands on the other side. The air was hazy and brownish. A thin trail led down into a wooded area. I wanna go there, Jamyang said, and so Wade took him into the trees, along a dry creek bed. Three small bikes were parked there, but Wade saw no sign of the children or drug dealers who would fit on them. There was a poster on a tree, however, that warned of a rapist who had been active in the area. A vague-looking man in a ski mask was pictured. Wade's ski mask was shoved into his jacket pocket, and he felt he was in danger. He imagined the owners of these bikes bound and gagged, and this excited him briefly, and then it just seemed trite and unworkable. Jamyang was nodding off on his shoulder, but then insisted that Wade put him down. They walked together to rejoin the main group, but Jamyang was dragging. He kept dropping his bottle, but refused to let Wade carry it for him.

I admire your entrepreneurial spirit, the sugar daddy was saying to Dhoji. But can't you come up with a business that doesn't involve your ex-husband shooting you up with drugs?

It seemed that Dhoji was renting out her womb. A wealthy Turkish couple was paying her to let them impregnate her with their fertilized eggs, but she had to shoot up hormones every day, so her body wouldn't reject the alien embryos. Now that she was fighting with Ricky, she had no one to give her the shots.

If I have to I can do it myself, she said. I was junkie in Delhi but I never shoot it. You been to India? Delhi is too much, it is too hot, you just wanna be junkie or something.

Wade could see that she had once been very pretty, but guessed that the hormones were bloating her, and ruining her skin. A woman jogged past, and smiled at the babies.

They walked off the main path, up through muddy fields. Cows backed away in terror, and the children screamed in terror and glee. Salah was talking about some "radical faeries" who'd originally invited him to live in the Bay Area in their "commune," which had been misrepresented and unsatisfying. David Baldhead was talking to Ralph about the fabulous Indian city of Dharamsala, where the Dalai Lama lived. Dhoji was talking about when she was a child at her Tibetan girls' school and they'd make her stand with her urine-soaked mattress on her head any time she wet the bed.

The light was fading. Jamyang sat on a log, and looked suddenly so over it all. He dropped his bottle, and it rolled down the hill through the mud. The talking trailed off, and Dhoji wandered off to have a cigarette. Wade sat on the log and waited for this moment to pass, this bubble of emptiness and futility that had welled up inside the afternoon. There was nothing to do but wait. Somebody was back behind him in the trees, some man or woman or child, and they were making the oddest noise. Wade couldn't decide if they were laughing or sobbing. He sat and waited, and tried to determine which it was.

IT WAS CLEAR TO WADE THAT DHOJI WAS TIRED OF LAMONT, BUT she wanted to go to Las Vegas. He couldn't tell how Lamont felt about Dhoji, but Lamont needed a place to stay, and didn't press the issue. In Las Vegas, Lamont slept in a room with his grandmother and his Auntie Vera and his sister, while Wade and the rock guy shared a room with Dhoji and the kids.

Las Vegas was cold.

Lamont's grandmother and Dhoji loved to play the slots, but everyone else was bored. Wade watched as Dhoji manically fed nickels into two different machines.

The sugar daddy suggested they see the sights. With Lamont's Auntie Vera and sister, and the two children, they wandered through the casinos. Two aged queens who'd endured far too many surgeries loomed over the city on a billboard with their white tiger, like archdemons presiding over one of the more painful levels of punishment. The sights of Las Vegas were uniformly bleak. The fake New York, the fake Venice. At the fake New York Wade heard a woman saying, You know how many kids are abducted by strangers every year? How many, somebody said. Like zero, said the woman. I mean really, almost none. At the fake Venice, the sugar daddy insisted on speaking Italian phrases, although nobody present understood a word. Outside of the Mandalay Bay, an old man was telling a woman who looked to be about ninety that he was getting tired of her friend Tina. It seemed that Tina was his woman, but he told the ninety-year-old that her friend Tina could be a real bitch.

Who do you think you are? said the old woman. Who do you think you are to talk about Tina that way?

She stepped back and narrowed her eyes at the old drunk.

Don't you know I have *things* in my bag, she said, and I will cut you?

THE OLD MAN BACKED DOWN. WADE AND HIS ENTOURAGE SHUF-
fled through the hotel lobby and out back into the garden.

The light was liquid gold. The shimmering gold surface of the
casino reflected it throughout the garden so that the sun seemed
muted, lovely, and unreal in the sky and the world itself a beautifully
illuminated stage encased in amber. Amber; that had been Auntie
Vera's stage name, once upon a time. They had always been wandering through this gold light in a dream. Auntie Vera was seventy, wore
a huge platinum-blonde wig. She'd had some showbiz career in the
fifties, and then gone crazy. She was an airy, gentle spirit with a gold,
starred tooth, floating through this false world like an apparition. She
was genteel, oblique, and hard as tacks. As soon as Jamyang shit his
diaper, she demurely handed the boy to Wade.

It was so cold. This light was perhaps the only beautiful thing
in this hellish city, but it was enough. The light forgave everything.
The light revealed these strangers he had fallen in with as strangers,
and sufficient in their silence and disgruntlement and shitty diapers.
Being a stranger was a complicated pleasure; this was the reason to
seek people out—because he didn't feel like he was one of them. If this
pleasure eventually became tiresome, he would find another way to
live. The sun was slowly setting in the west; the light was fading.

AT THAT HOUSE, HE HAD WANDERED INTO A DARK AND EMPTY bedroom where a movie played on the VCR. A harried blonde woman was trying to make sense of her life, in a world that was occasionally bleached of its sound and vitality, even its ability to see her. She was located halfway between two worlds. Reality flickered in and out. She was in a mechanic's garage, trapped in a jacked-up automobile, and some ghoul was perhaps approaching. Wade had felt briefly and bizarrely that he had always been watching that film. That he had dreamed it once, and forever. The woman was already dead, but in denial.

BACK IN THE CASINO, NOTHING HAD CHANGED. DHOJI WAS almost out of money, and a weary desperation was creeping into the edges of their little social grouping. Wade just wanted to play the slots. Instead, he handed the baby he was carrying to the sugar daddy and walked into the horrible cold and past a pirate ship battle and down the Strip to the edge of town. It was almost dark now, and utterly without warmth. He took off his shirt and put on his ski mask and stood by the highway leading out of this place, waiting for someone to take him away.

Next to him was an Adopt-a-Highway sign, and he remembered that someone had once run over some children who'd been cleaning this road. He had never known any boys who'd adopted a highway, and he was glad of that.

His nipples were startling and human. This invitation to all the most reckless possible sequences was an act of war. His face was the face of murder. The people in cars didn't seem quite as surprised as he was himself. Murder and rape were such predictable ways of being a monster; he wanted to be a monster of freedom: a complex freedom and mask and empathy that wasn't obligatory and wasn't violence. He would give anybody who chose him whatever horror or game it was they wanted; he wanted to use up all the horrors and all the games until he was simply an empty space where something had happened. A familiar car pulled over. He was curious to see what kind of psychopath had answered the invitation.

It was the Italian. It seemed the sugar daddy, Mr. Tan Slacks, was an old friend, and he'd kept the Italian abreast of all Wade's movements. Wade was surprised. He hadn't at all felt like he was being pursued. There should have been clues—hushed phone conversations in the next room, encrypted messages—and most importantly a pervasive feeling that somebody or some *thing* was closing in on him.

You're quite the detective, said Wade.

He meant by this that the man was ridiculous and distracted from his own pathology by meaningless clues.

I am in love with you, the Italian told him. His use of language disgusted Wade. Everything they had shared was being cheapened with stock phrases. Wade found his melodrama exhausting. He thought their culture was famous for it. He'd heard of a famous Italian director who got run over by some rough trade.

There was something inherently funny about "getting run over," but he couldn't remember where he'd acquired this odd idea. The Italian insisted they set up a tent in the desert. He kept beginning his sentences with the word "you." You are the most savage beauty, you are the one I have been looking for, etc. The Italian was entranced by brutal American nature, and wanted his sexual and landscape metaphors to converge. He wanted to be fucked in a tent.

WEST CITY POLICE DEPARTMENT
POLYGRAPH REPORT
To: Det. R.

Purpose of Examination: Homicide investigation
In the Pretest Interview, the subject denied having
been in the woods behind the Bluebird Motel on the date
of the murder. Subject denied being present when victim
was killed and denied having killed victim. Also said
did not know who killed victim.

A 10 question polygraph test was formulated and three
polygraph charts were conducted. The test contained the
following relevant questions:
Q3 At any time Wed or Wed night were you in the woods
"No"
Q5 Were you present when the victim was killed "No"
Q7 Did you kill the victim "No"
Q8 Do you know who killed the victim "No"
Q10 Do you suspect anyone of having killed the victim.
"No"

It is the opinion of this polygraph examiner that this
subject recorded significant responses indicative
of deception when answering above listed relevant
questions in the manner noted.

CONCLUSION: Deception indicated. In the post-test
interview, subject denied any involvement in this
crime. After approximately 45 minutes I asked the
subject what were they afraid of, Subject replied
"The Electric Chair." After a short period of time,
the subject ceased to deny involvement in the crime.
(Admission through: Absence of Denial.) Subject then
said, "I will tell you all about it, if you let me talk
to my mother." (Subject's real mother had been dead for
many years.)

Report #5

SUSPECT'S ITEMS: Two notebooks that appeared to have
Satanic or cult writings in them, a red T-shirt,

blue jeans, and boots were taken from Suspect's
backpack. One, containing his collection of poetry
and "stories" and quotations, was introduced into
court. The other, if it is not somehow related to
the first, (as suggested by an example: when first
booked, his arrest report listed among his personal
effects a pair of shoelaces, neglecting to point out
that they were the shoelaces laced into his boots, not
something separate), remains a mystery. The introduced
journal contained morbid images and references to
dead children, as well as an eclectic hodgepodge
of quotations from the likes of Bad Food songs and
Henri Michaux, mixed in with Suspect's own moody "gay
angst" style writing. It contained a sort of "life
history" filled with clearly false information; for
example, Suspect clearly did NOT grow up in the state
he claimed. The process of trying to pin down direct
correspondences with characters and events in Suspect's
life was virtually fruitless, given both confusions in
the "stories" and in Suspect's life history. Despite
gaps in the so-called narrative the abundance of
references to molested and/or murdered children was
deemed relevant by the state. The trial court allowed
the State to introduce entries containing images of
death, as well as references to rotting flesh and dead
children. The State focused upon an entry that said
"I want to be in the middle. In neither the black nor
the white. In neither the wrong nor the right." The
State offered the statement to explain the confusion
expressed by the occult expert, Dr. G., that some
of the symbols in one of Suspect's books were from
the Wiccan, or "white magic" religion, and others
from Satanism, or "black magic," and the two are not
consistent.

The red T-shirt was taken for the same reason as
Suspect's lover's robe. The trial court also allowed
in evidence items taken from Suspect's backpack.
These items included a dog's skull; an instruction
manual to a car alarm; a funeral register upon which
Suspect had drawn a pentagram and upside-down crosses
and had copied various spells; a heavy-metal poster

depicting graveyards; a skateboard magazine; newspaper
clippings concerning the recent and as yet unsolved
case (presumed to be a homicide) in which a hotel room
downtown was discovered with its walls smeared with
excrement and blood; and torn pictures of the lead
singer of a little-known indie band.

There was additional evidence presented by the state or
elicited from witnesses intending to show that Suspect
delved deeply into the occult:
* The fact that Suspect read books by Anton LaVey (the
founder of the modern Church of Satan, which does NOT
advocate human sacrifice), horror novelist Stephen
King, and one tome called "This Tree Grows Out of Hell"
about Aztec and Maya human sacrifice and cosmology.
* Det. R's expert testimony that these kinds of reading
materials are "strange" for someone of Suspect's age
and social position.
* The fact that Suspect was at least familiar via
secondhand research with the theories of Aleister
Crowley, a turn of the century occultist/magician whose
writings seem to advocate--arguably in a tongue-in-
cheek manner, according to scholars--human sacrifice.

Report #10

Dr. G., an expert in occult killings, testified that
the killing had the "trappings of occultism." He
testified that the date of the killings, near a pagan
holiday, was significant, as well as the fact that
there was a full moon. He stated that young children
are often sought for sacrifice because "the younger,
the more innocent, the better the life force." He
testified that sacrifices are often done near water
for a baptism-type rite or just to wash the blood
away. The fact that the victim was tied ankle to wrist
was significant because this was done to display the
genitalia. He stated that the absence of blood at the
scene could be significant because cult members store
blood for future services in which they would drink the
blood or bathe in it. He testified that the "overkill"
or multiple cuts could reflect occult overtones. Dr. G.

testified that there was significance in injuries to
the left side of the victims as distinguished from the
right side: people who practice occultism will use the
midline theory, drawing straight down through the body.
The right side is related to those things synonymous
with Christianity while the left side is that of the
practitioners of the satanic occult. He testified
that the clear place on the bank could be consistent
with a ceremony. In sum, Dr. G. testified there was
significant evidence of satanic ritual killings. Under
cross-examination, it was revealed that Dr. G. had
received his doctorate from a mail-order University.
When asked if the opposite of the conditions in which
the body was found had been the case (for instance,
if the victim had not been found near water, had not
been tied ankle to wrist), Dr. G. answered that those
conditions could also be related to satanic activity.

ONE WINTER HE CAMPED IN THE MOUNTAINS ABOVE LOS ANGELES.
A poster warned him and his latest friend that out in the brush, in the
dark, were the Africanized bees. Their story was heroic; the original
bees had been taken to Brazil for research purposes, to see about giving
the local bees more pep. The queen herself had effected a daring escape
from the lab, and the rest was history. Mountain ranges couldn't stop
them. Eventually they'd cover the hemisphere.

Wade was kept awake through the night by a bear, stomping
around the campground, beating on cars and garbage cans. Dogs
barked. In the morning Wade discovered that a small strip of plastic
had been ripped off the car. He was tiring of the whole nature thing.
There were just as many rules and borders, and these disturbing families with walkie-talkies and military outfits, marching their children
through the trees. He needed a good night's rest. When he opened the
car trunk to get at a pair of warmer socks, a rodent peered up at him
and vanished deeper into the trunk. Mice were frowned on these days,
because of viruses that would make people bleed in unusual ways. He
reached for his clothes, to move them somewhere else, and screamed.
The mouse had given birth in his underwear. The offspring were three
in number, and blind. There was something unfinished about them,
as of a gel or an organ. They merely squirmed as he removed boxers
and babies together and dropped them on the open ground. The food
chain was supposed to be beautiful, co-evolutionary, but up close and
personal it was too much.

You look like you've had it, his lover said.

Wade was speechless. It was like a mobile venereal disease had
rooted in his drawers. Their mother was still somewhere in the inner
workings of the car. He could hear her squeaking as they drove down
the mountain.

At a rest stop along I-5 a sign warned them that the rodents here
had plague. If you developed certain symptoms, you were to be sure to
inform your doctor that you'd been in a plague area.

L.A. was a relief. There was such a haze across the sky it seemed a
catastrophe was on-going. Pearl grey doesn't suit you? his lover said.
Wade felt as if his lungs were filling with blood. He was home and safe
again inside a vast loneliness.

ON THEIR WAY THROUGH THE BAY AREA, THEY STOPPED IN TO
see Dhoji. She had just returned from Vermont. An older Tibetan man
had flown her out, but Dhoji said he was just too ugly, so she'd taken
the bus to visit friends in Boston and New York. Otherwise, she'd just
finished her first lesbian affair, which hadn't worked out either. She'd
miscarried the Turkish couple's embryo, gotten off the hormones and
slimmed down. The children looked just like he would have guessed—
extrapolations of their previous forms. He could tell they didn't remember him, even though Dhoji pretended that they did.

The children were anxious about the possibility of mommy marry-
ing a black guy, as their daddy's girlfriend had told them that black
guys carried guns, that black guys were dangerous.

Anyway, said Dhoji. Only one they know who really have gun is
d-a-d-d-y.

WADE AND HIS LOVER STAYED IN A CABIN BY THE OCEAN NORTH of San Francisco. The dark came early, and the rain. This one wanted to know about Wade's feelings. He was insistent. Wade talked about riding his bike down the highways in the wind. He told the man about his mother's death, and that afterwards his father had walked out onto the land and never returned. Did you sell the farm? asked his lover. Wade nodded. That was the simplest explanation. Wade told him about a movie he'd once seen, about a man with X-ray eyes. Experiments designed to enable more seeing had created conflict with deluded authorities, an accidental murder, refuge with society's carnival outcasts as a prescient freak and jaded healer, and then a journey to Las Vegas . . . to peer into its cold, hellish heart . . . and a final revelatory flight into the desert. The man stumbled into a revival meeting, with its silly proclamations of sin and salvation. Saved? No, he didn't want to be saved. He just wanted to tell them what he'd *seen*. Vast darknesses as large as time itself . . . and beyond that . . .

His lover asked him if he'd ever set fires as a boy.

Only once, said Wade.

What did you burn? asked his lover.

Just an old shirt, said Wade. I didn't want to wear those old hand-me-downs anymore, so I tried to burn it in the stove.

Little fashion queen, said his lover. How touching. That's the only time?

Once in the fields, said Wade. But that was an accident. I was trying to send a smoke signal.

His lover didn't believe that there were accidents, an idea that seemed so extreme to Wade that it wasn't worth refuting. He asked Wade about his first love. Wade had never told anyone about that man in the tub. There was this teenager I bought a bike from, he said. He raped me. I mean, not really, but that's what he called it. He sat me naked on the bicycle seat, bent over, hanging onto the handlebars. I kept going back for more. Back in the trees once, he kissed me.

Wade didn't think his lover believed him. He didn't think his lover believed you could get fucked on a bicycle.

There were blue flowers, he said.

Wade knew that what he told about his childhood wasn't exactly possible. He realized he wanted to go into the woods with this man and come out with someone different. He realized he was addicted to certain feelings, kept going after them time and time again. Arriving in a strange city at night. Tying complicated knots and then abandoning them. Ass fucking. He appreciated a certain amount of struggle in that regard, and a disparity in power. He enjoyed finding it when he'd been looking for it. Or else exhausting himself and then climbing a hill in some city to look over the landscape . . . as if the landscape was the body of his struggle and exhaustion redeemed. It wasn't. But uselessness could always be a glory of its own. He wanted to try something new. But novelty itself participated in a particular mood . . .

There was nothing to do through the evening in the cabin but make love and then feed the fire and listen to the ocean and pass in and out of half sleep. He dreamed that he woke in the night and saw a clown on a rooftop with a child. He dreamed of a coastal town where huge mounds of trash were being sold to tourists. He dreamed of a rat-faced boy from junior high who had briefly befriended him, and then betrayed him. How odd. He lay awake then, remembering. He hadn't thought about that boy in years. He'd forgotten that boy had ever walked upon the earth.

IN THE MORNING THEY WENT INTO THE NEAREST TOWN, WHERE old hippies and potters lived with goats. At the grocer's, women sniffed organic pears intimately, smugly, and then put them back in the pile with the rest. Wade and his lover had coffee and scones and rummaged through a pile of free clothes.

Late in the afternoon, they returned to the cabin and walked some ways down the beach. The beach was empty, and the tide coming in. They scrambled over rocks. At an outcropping where a thin creek tumbled down the cliffside, they climbed up along beside it. It was getting cold, and Wade was ready to go back, so he hurried past his friend, and across the stream. He wanted to hasten the moment when they could either go no further, or from which they could at least see that there wasn't any reason to go further. He crossed over the stream and started down the cliff on the other side. As he stepped onto and off a large boulder, things tumbled underneath him.

HE WAS CLINGING TO A ROCK, AND HE COULDN'T MOVE HIS right leg. The large boulder was on top of his heel. His friend looked panicked.

Stay there, he said. Don't move.

He hurried across the stream or creek toward him.

I can't move, Wade said.

His foot was being smashed into the front of the shoe and his ankle had been scraped; it hurt. His friend was concerned that other rocks above him might come loose and kill him. This is a serious situation, he said.

They examined the foot, but couldn't tell if the rock was actually crushing part of the heel, or just the heel of the shoe. Either way, the boulder was too large to move, and there was no way to get the foot out of the shoe. There was nothing to do but get help. Don't move anything, his friend told him. He looked anxiously at the rocks above, and then hurried down the cliff and up the beach for help.

OKAY, WADE SAID. HE WAS ODDLY RELIEVED TO BE ALONE. HE wasn't sure how bad this pain was. It ebbed. It certainly wasn't debilitating. He tried not to think about it. His friend climbed an outcropping of rocks, disappeared on the other side, and the ocean was streaked with silver. The sky was clouding up, and the clouds had a darkness to them, as of rain.

There was a brightness to the edges of the material world, and an insignificance that elated him. He wondered if he was having an endorphin rush. He didn't feel like he was having an endorphin rush, but he laughed. His toes were crushed into the front of the shoe, and there was some tingling, as of an impending numbness, and there was pain. He could barely wiggle them, and wondered if some were broken. He tried to look at his situation as an exercise in problem solving. If he was alone here, without the prospect of help, what might he do to free himself? Would he just linger here and die? He didn't have any matches in his pocket, or a knife. He had money, and tissue, and lint.

TWO HIKERS SCRAMBLED OVER THE ROCKS BENEATH HIM, A MAN
and a woman. Hello, he said. The woman looked up at him and gave a
polite smile. I'm stuck under this rock, he told her, but help is on its
way. Oh, she said, without slowing down, Are you okay? Oh, sure, he
said.

They proceeded down the beach. There wasn't really anything for
them to do, but still. He couldn't imagine that he would ever treat a
man pinned to the earth so cavalierly.

GARBAGE WAS STUCK IN THE ROCKS BY THE STREAM. NOTHING that seemed useful or entertaining or that he could reach. The significant moments of his life should stand out in startling clarity, he decided, and he should realize the crucial connections between events, past and future. He remembered that flannel bush.

He'd fallen in with a man who owned a pickup truck. They'd driven back into the hills where the rich people lived, startled to discover huge estates tucked into the mountains, but overlooking the ocean. It was Super Sunday on tv, a corrupt and clueless sort of family, with dogs. The woman showed them the bush they'd agreed to haul away for fifty dollars, and then explained the highly toxic nature of a flannel bush; it would eat away their clothes and irritate their skin. They'd been conned by this woman, but there was no turning back; it had taken them a half hour just to find the place, and they needed the money. The bush did in fact destroy their jeans and their shirts and their gloves, and they dumped it somewhere along the side of the road.

The issue was killing time until he was rescued. Distracting himself from pain and circulating his thoughts. Once he'd put this all behind him, he thought he'd do some spontaneous and joyful things. He refused to crush that comforting thought with the weight of the specific. He remembered something that went "Rest in my arms until the world's crying is over." It was probably a Jesus thing, but he preferred to think of those arms as the hum of an electric dishwasher. He used to curl up next to it on cold nights, for the heat it gave off and for the comforting vibrations. Once, in a town by the mountains, he waited under a gas station awning, and the rain was coming in. The air had been warm and dark. Once as a child he'd done a project out of melted crayons. He thought that it was referred to as "wax resist." He wanted to spout gibberish at those passersby. Ha, ha, ha, he wanted to say. Oh, you don't get it, he wanted to tell them. Nobody gets it, nobody but me. Pain can make you smug and self-righteous, he realized. Those people were long gone anyway. An airplane appeared in the sky, to his left, just at the edge of his vision. Airplanes in the sky had never ceased to look outrageous, and impossibly real. Oh, the structures of the world weren't so scary. The power grids, the robots, the wiping clean. Compartments and nonsense. When they'd sent those first men to the moon, the president had prepared a speech for the possibility that they'd get stuck up there. That they wouldn't be able to return. The speech praised their bravery and sacrifice, but expressed no regret.

He wondered if he might soon be enduring worse pain. If so, he guessed he would simply do it.

PROBABLY, ALL THE STORIES ENDED UP HERE, BY THE WESTERN ocean. He didn't know what he meant by that. Maybe he'd limited his own possibilities by believing that in some way. On the one hand, it was really beautiful. On the other, he was bored.

Danger is fun, he thought. On the other hand, too much danger is simply a chore.

THERE'D BEEN A PERIOD IN HIS LIFE . . . A TIME . . . HE'D BEEN interested in human children raised by wolves. But he couldn't remember any of the interesting facts. They'd been paraded around and reabsorbed and lived tragic lives, he guessed. In between cultures. He was relieved that his suffering, when he had suffered, hadn't meant anything. It hadn't purchased anything. He wasn't sure he'd ever suffered before, but this certainly qualified. That fact made him happy in a diffused way; now he was really existing. The insubstantiality he'd felt in the world, as if he was a breeze or an afterthought, was tempered by this new reality. Now he was a trapped animal. Wade was pleased that he had a definite place in the world, and that he didn't want to be there anymore: once he was free, he could wander and wander, and it would never feel like a curse. He'd heard rumors of a drought on the plains. He'd heard rumors that the white people and the farms were leaving, that the buffalo were coming back. He hoped it was true, that the land would simply erase the memory of what had happened on it: his childhood. He hoped the land would make itself strange. He was so bored. The pain in his foot and his leg just continued. He examined the foot, trying to figure out if the rock was on top of his ankle or not. If he was really into survival, he could always chew it off. The clouds were darkening and the air chilling, and he remembered how quickly weather sometimes changed, how he sat in less difficult circumstances and watched as it changed. Perhaps he'd been out in it, and so was deeply involved in the rate of a coming rain, and then it would seem to be dissipating, it wouldn't rain at all, but usually it rained and he got wet. He was pretty sure this was one of those times when it would rain. He might get hypothermia out here, or the stream might be transformed into a gushing cascade that would loosen rocks up above him and he'd be crushed. He didn't really believe it.

His friend had diagnosed him as a risk-taker. He thought that meant Wade had a death wish. But Wade had never wanted to die. He'd wanted to combat boredom sometimes, and to test his fate; to prove that he had a destiny and a specific death that suited him. He'd always wanted to go on a journey he'd never return from. If the only such journey most people could imagine was death, that wasn't his problem. There were islands out there to the west. You'd pass through a fog. You'd sleep on the boat until your consciousness was no different from the mist. Whatever it was the mist wanted, you would want that too.

He'd once felt like he had "regrets." But now it seemed that there was only one road, and it looked like the ocean underneath the sky. Everything happened on that road, sooner or later.

SOME MYTH DESCRIBED A SIMILAR SITUATION, HE BELIEVED, some myth involving the concept of "forever." He didn't know any myths. Shouldn't he be learning something? The lesson was that he was pinned to the earth; that he couldn't fly. Hadn't he already known that? The ocean was absolutely huge out there, and it looked cold and wet. The world was huge, and time was huge, but maybe not his. On the other hand, maybe he'd live through a nightmare, freezing and crushed in the rain. The metaphor of being "pinned to the earth" was bad enough, but the lived reality was horrible. He studied the garbage in the stream again. In a crevice to his right there was a pair of jeans that might have belonged to a boy, or to a small woman. He couldn't see anything wrong with them. People were so wasteful, and he was glad of that. He watched the airplane just now disappearing from his sight. He closed his eyes and wasn't anywhere that had any relation to his life—it was as if he was another person, and not one he had anything much in common with. He searched for a specific memory he could tie clearly to his own self. In Las Vegas, there had been nothing anywhere except clanging bells and machinery designed to take people's money.

He stood behind Dhoji and tried to be entertained by the prospect of three BARs aligning. Somewhere nearby, bells were going off and change was pouring into somebody's coffers. He had looked around and seen that everyone was wearing identical expressions, as if they were all taking the same meds. It might have been the middle of the afternoon, or it might have been the middle of the night. A woman wore a gown. The rock guy handed him a roll of quarters, and Wade fed them into the machines and pulled the lever and fed and pulled and fed and pulled.

The goal of all this was eluding him, but he managed to care somehow that he win enough to keep going. He tried to pay attention to his own mental state as he pulled and fed. He could be waiting for a bus. Not the bus that collected him every morning of his boyhood, but a bus in a mountain city, at a downtown transit center, where teenagers smoked cigarettes and illegal immigrants told stoic jokes. It occurred to him that human life had ended a long time ago and nobody noticed. This thought participated in a weird and certainly false nostalgia for values that annoyed him. In any case, nothing had preceded this moment. These machines had always been here under this sick lighting. If you tried to trace them backward through time, if you tried to remember the origin of these mechanisms, you would never emerge anywhere. You would always be inside a casino. Wade guessed that none of this made sense, except to reptiles; and he was a reptile. Those dusty afternoons in the farmhouse attic as a child he had already experienced eternity, so that what he had come to think of as the world—a place where people did things to each other and their names circulated through time like money—he could relegate no more importance than a vague ashy sensation on the tip of his tongue. He had met hard, sunburnt western women, skinny, in tight jeans. They had the faces and asses of men, but with frills pasted onto their hair and their blouses, to tell the world they were girls. He had met young men who talked always about meerkats and living in a yurt and surfing in Indonesia. Either they had surfed in Indonesia or somebody they knew and admired had surfed in Indonesia, they thought that meerkats were badass, they plotted the purchase of a yurt for some cheap land somewhere. They all knew how to beat a urine test, and how to beat a lie detector, by clenching your sphincter muscle. Wade laughed at the thought of his "crime." Then he wasn't sure if it was as funny as all that. There was no way to know if it was a joke, perhaps, or if he had in fact wandered into some sinister sex-and-murder business of the sort that everyone imagined record producers were up to out there in the hills in California. Either that house was a place of sophisticated pleasures and freedoms, of volunteers, or it was a brutal world of sadism, injustice, murder, and confusion. He kept feeding quarters into the machine. A teenage girl two slots over was talking earnestly with a man who looked like her father. I don't think shame is all bad, she was saying. I think some people should feel ashamed. The expressions on her face and the man's didn't change. In books he'd read as a child, there had been wild animals, mysteries, jungles, inexplicable customs. It seemed there was none of that left. Yet every day there was more "nothing." He'd often made peace with the destruction of the land, water, air, animals, and most of the people. He'd guessed it was simply a reality you had to adjust to or use for something spectacular. But he'd wake up and discover that no nadir had actually been reached yet, that the process of bottoming out, as a species, had only just begun. These people want an end to their stories, Wade thought. It wasn't the girl and her father he meant by "these people," it was "everybody," or else the imaginary people who had decided that human life could look the way it looked in that endless room of carpets and mirrors. They pretended it was dangerous and exciting, but it was only new. On the other hand, these thoughts all felt predictable. He felt like everyone thought these things in Las Vegas, and then they were so overwhelmed by despair that they gave up, emptied their minds. He got a rhythm and a pace going with the quarters, so that it was like he and the machine were the same thing, and this rhythm was a satisfying replacement for thinking. Down to his last few quarters, he began to feel a dim panic that consciousness was going to re-enter his life. The last quarter went in, and then he was alone in eternity, face-to-face with a useless machine. He turned to look for someone he knew.

Children and whores, had he never known anyone else? Were there other categories? He saw his friend far off down the beach, just now climbing up the cliffside toward the cabins. His progress was incredibly slow. Wade began singing quietly, to the tune of a song he knew as a child. The song was about silver and gold and came from a winter tv special. This special involved misfits on a journey to an island of unwanted toys. Most of the characters were thinly veiled homosexuals. But instead of "silver and gold," Wade sang "children and whores, children and whores." He remembered the way Dhoji's children had pointed at things and demanded things and put on a show, pretending that the mermaid Barbie doll was a microphone. They sang songs about jumping on beds or songs about spiders on rainspouts. Was there a distinction between children and whores? Wade decided that pain was making him cynical. His friend hadn't even arrived yet, and this meant that Wade had spent less than half the time under this rock that he would spend. "Less than half" was a far too generous way of thinking about it, he realized. People would have to be called, they would have to arrive, and finally, they would have to do something. He couldn't imagine what that would be.

HE HAD BECOME A PLACE. A LONGITUDE, A LATITUDE, AN ASPECT of the weather. Different entities assembled sometimes. Splitting apart and recombining and veering toward a limit. He could be interrogated, forced to piece together something or other. Do you see me more as a mineral or as plant life? he would ask. Stratified or rooted? The detective would get irritated. Stick to the facts, he'd say.

Where did you get your money during this time?

How exactly do you live?

Where have you been, exactly?

Did you light fires as a boy?

Do bicycle seats excite you sexually?

What kind of a monster are you?

Fortunately, he'd never be interrogated. Being pinned to the earth was a replacement, he thought, for interrogation. The two were mutually exclusive. Or maybe being pinned to the earth was instead an alibi. *I am not where you think I am. I am where you think I am not.* If he was etheric and abstract, he could be elsewhere simultaneously, murdering or what-have-you, seducing children into the "homosexual lifestyle," but they'd never be able to pin it on him. He remembered that storm he had seen once over the ocean. It wasn't that he had caused the storm, as it had seemed to him then, that the storm was a reflection of his own mood and desires. It wasn't either that the storm had shaped his mood, so that he could recognize himself in the weather. Rather, the storm and his mood had co-evolved.

He felt like he used that word too much. He lacked a firm grasp of evolutionary theory, to be throwing around that concept whenever it popped into his head. Maybe it hadn't been a storm at all, but an enormous fogbank he'd mistaken for a storm. But hadn't there been lightning? If there had been lightning, it would imply boys. Boys in the woods? Something was hungry for them, something both human and weather. He would never know for sure. A boy riding a bike down a dusty highway. A breeze and a beating sun. On the other hand, a girl. She's on a boat. The fog and the foghorns and the ice. Oh, a pirate. *I am to be a pirate, a foghorn, a pterodactyl, a ghost, a machine . . .* If he was to witness the oscillations that went on and on and on, ocean-like, the infinity of gods, the heartbeat of enveloping eternity . . . he guessed his jaw would simply drop. It wouldn't be a surprise, but it would be joyful and calming. On the other hand, it wouldn't do him any good. His foot hurt. It hurt and hurt and hurt and hurt. After emerging from the luscious hell of that world, the world of ferns and molecules and carnivorous lizards and spiders, after discovering the unnecessariness of everything that is "face" . . . there'd still be a luxury and a profoundly decorative sensuality in what he'd come to think of as being human: empathy, tenderness, lust, and abstract thinking. Morality and murdering children.

ONCE, HE'D BOUGHT A GLUE TRAP, ALTHOUGH HE'D BEEN WARNED they were a vile business. He'd thought he was up for torturing a mouse. He'd only wanted it to go away. Hadn't he tried filling its little mouse holes with SOS pads? Instead of packing up and moving on, it became glued, squeaking, panicked. Desperately ripping its own innards out in a terrified attempt to free itself from its own body. He'd put it into a paper bag, taken it out back and dropped a rock on it.

Nobody had, of course, dropped this rock on his heel. This was clear to him, at least, while he was pinned to the earth. The world contained too many animal species for each of them to contain a lesson. Bats like winged foxes with enormous webby ears. Green lacewing larvae fed on meat until they grew up to eat only nectar and pollen. His friend had told him about the relish with which his mother sought out stories of dogs that turned on their masters. It happened surprisingly often, and was reported in the news. Mountain lions, on the other hand, were hunted and killed whenever they snacked on human pets.

THE GREAT DIE-OFF. SLAUGHTERHOUSES AND PICNICS. MAD COW disease.

If he was to stay with this man, this lover, who was now off some-where involved in the whole abstract business of rescue . . . He was glad that at least it hadn't fallen on him to do the rescuing. That he didn't have to explain to anyone the mechanics of how exactly he was pinned to the earth. Although maybe precision wasn't required in such a case. Still, the process of mobilization itself seemed embarrassing.

HE REMEMBERED HE USED TO BE FRIGHTENED OF DEATH. HE'D done exercises to help him overcome the fear. None of them worked, but now it seemed that he wasn't afraid. He'd been alive for such a long, long time.

He couldn't imagine living again the time he had spent here. If he got out of this "situation," one of these days he'd have a good cry. And then, sometime, he'd just disperse. His breath would fly from his lungs and he would soar for one instant over the earth. He'd participate in a vast sensation of freedom and wisdom, he guessed, and then he'd be gone and never come back. Was it the moment of death that interested him? Probably it didn't quite work that way. There were no words for it. "Gone" was still a state, "back" a place, "never" a relationship of time. It couldn't be imagined, not really, but then people just kept on doing it, over and over again.

IF HE WAS TO STAY WITH THIS MAN, ONE OF THEM WOULD HAVE
to watch the other one die. As life progressed, there was this dying
along with this witnessing of the dying. It was a form of torture, interwoven with the other bits, the bits that weren't torture. Once, he'd
had lists of things to do in the day, and had crossed items off that list.

They had agreed to love. Or something. To witness each other's
deaths. If you could fully experience the depth of the sadness, something new might grow out of the cavity where your heart had been.
Unless this was just a game designed to make unbearable sadness seem
like it had a use; to make it bearable. He would die and his friend
would die, but they wouldn't die together.

These thoughts were doing their job, that was all, the current job of
all of his thoughts, which was to distract him from pain. He wished he
was sexually excited, but he was too cold. Abstraction wasn't enough.
He examined the plant life in his immediate vicinity, and once again,
the garbage. Could you still distinguish between the two, nature and
garbage? A rare bird, an old couple with binoculars, a Pennzoil can
from 1962, an obsolete computer monitor.

OFF IN THE DISTANCE, MEN WERE SCURRYING DOWN THE CLIFFSIDE.

The experience of "relief being in sight" sped up his sensation of time. He now allowed himself to imagine that point when he wouldn't be in pain anymore, and when he'd be able to move. Instead of just accentuating his pain, these thoughts actually worked to relieve it. It hadn't rained after all.

THE FIRST MEMBER OF THE RESCUE SQUAD GAVE WADE HIS FIRE coat. Warmth alone flooded him with euphoria. Everything these men said made him giggle. He wasn't at all embarrassed by being cared for.

He was surrounded by men in firemen's outfits. It was a heavy boulder, and they were thrilled by the prospect of airlifting him out of there. Meanwhile, the Emergency Medical Technician, a spiffy gay man, was calmly and methodically cutting Wade's pantleg off, and then cutting off his shoe with the sharpest of scissors. He'd already relieved so much pressure that Wade felt reborn. The other men were speaking into their walkie-talkies, strategizing elaborate maneuvers involving bracing mechanisms to hold back the rocks above, chains, and at least two helicopters, when the front of his shoe fell away and Wade's foot was freed.

The men packed up their things, disappointed. Wade left his pantleg there in the stream, but took his shoe with him, as his lover helped him hobble barefoot down the beach.

Offender Psychological Profile (continued)

This will be an extremely egocentric individual who
cannot take the criticism of others, or tolerate
shortcomings of any kind. He will require instant
gratification, and react violently when impulses
are not satisfied. He is glib and superficial, but
also extremely manipulative. He must be dominant
in all relationships with women. His jealousy and
possessiveness can and have manifested themselves in
violent behavior acted out towards the females in his
life.

Arrest History
The numerous precautionary actions taken by the
offender, despite the fact the crime was not
planned fully, demonstrate a level of knowledge
and sophistication obtained through either repeated
offenses, some level of exposure to law enforcement
training and techniques, or previous arrests for
similar crimes. The offender shows some knowledge of
forensic methods, and attempts to dupe those specific
efforts. Has very possibly spent time in prison, or
is committing other petty crimes to support himself.
He will most likely have been arrested or detained
for incidents involving drugs, violent behavior, and
assaultive behavior.

Residence
The offender lives within a few miles of the disposal
site. This is indicated by the very poor attempt at
concealing the body when disposing of it, and the
fact that it was disposed of where it would be quickly
found, in the area being searched by so many people
including law enforcement. It is likely, in fact, that
the offender was part of the search effort, and that he
placed the body in a specific location with the intent
of being the one to later find it in an attempt to
shift the blame.

Skill Level
It is not likely that the offender is educated past
the high-school level. He would have performed poorly
in school due to his aggressive nature, intolerance
for others, and his overall impatience. He does not
demonstrate characteristics of education at the high
school level, though he may have obtained a GED at
some point. However the offender demonstrates a wealth
of applied criminal knowledge about investigative
techniques and forensic methods. He is not the kind of
offender to leave obvious physical evidence behind at
a crime scene without making some attempt to obscure
it.

Family History
Offender will have a background displaying a shortage
of males and sporadic contact with male authority
figures. (Experts agree that it is good to have a
male, especially for young boys.) Offender's mother
may have been a criminal herself, or a prostitute,
as it is known that criminal behavior often runs in
families.

Hobbies/ Personal Interests
As indicated by his use of one or more knives in
the commission of this crime, this offender has an
intense interest in knives and likely has an extensive
collection of them in his home. It is also likely
that the offender has the same type of interest in
firearms, and in hunting.

Employment
It is likely that this offender is unemployed. He
lacks the skills, discipline, and patience to hold
down a full-time job. When employed, he is often late,
absent, or fails to show up at all. His temper and
disposition keep him from legitimate work, and likely
his true source of income is the sale of drugs or
other illegal activity.

Transportation
If he does own a vehicle, it would be masculine, like a
truck. This would also be consistent with the type of
vehicle he would need to transport the victims to the
disposal site. It would further be in strict keeping
with his macho self-image of strength and control.

Based on this evidence, the location of the disposal
site, the victimology, and the other injuries inflicted
on the victim, it is the opinion of this examiner
that this case represents a battered child or child-
custodial homicide. To a greater extent the parents,
and to a lesser extent the guardians, relatives and
anyone else who was allowed frequent, trusted access
to this child should be thoroughly investigated as
suspects in this case.

INVESTIGATIVE REPORT
OFFENSE: Homicide

SUSPECT was apprehended in parking lot of Oceanside
Café. Jacket matched description given by Laurie L.
Denied involvement in CRIME. Suspect then said, "Look
at the ocean. It's vast." Asked to clarify, Suspect
said, "Big. It's real big."

PSYCH EXAM

Suspect's medical records contained the following
notations of statements by Suspect: I want to go where
the monsters go. Pretty much hate the human race.
Relates that people are in two classes, sheep and
wolves. Wolves eat sheep. Sometimes Suspect does "blow
up." Describes this as more than anger, like rage.
Relates that when this happens, the only solution is
to hurt someone. When questioned on feelings Suspect
states, "I know I'm going to influence the world.
People will remember me." Dr. M. strongly cautioned
against drawing conclusions from a small sampling
of Suspect's statements selected because of their

234 • STEPHEN BEACHY

ostensibly hostile, blood-oriented content. He argued
that they needed to be placed into their context to be
understood, and that the overall conclusions he drew
about Subject were quite different than one might make
by studying only these. Suspect's own claim is that
the most he ever did was "lick" a little blood from a
few people, mostly just for shock value... Regarding
Suspect's purported rage toward the doctor that treated
his mother, Dr. M stated, "Few dispute that the results
of Dr. R.'s treatment were months of unbearable agony
for Suspect's mother, suffering Suspect witnessed
firsthand as she approached her painful death." "I have
never seen a boy so ineffably saddened," the treating
doctor, Dr. R. was quoted. "Suspect's experience of his
mother's death," Dr. M stated, "looms behind his later
diatribes, and his use of words like poison, cancer,
and abscesses to describe the human race."

Report #14

At the time of Suspect's trial, his "confession"
conflicted with at least six known issues of fact.
a) Placing the victim out of school at time he was
demonstrably in school.
b) Stating victim was bound with rope whereas he was
found tied with his own shoelaces.
c) Stating boy was choked into unconsciousness with a
stick whereas the medical examiner could detect nothing
to indicate this.
d) Stating boy was "screwed," implying anal rape,
whereas medical examiner could find no signs of the
expected anal abrasions or other evidence which would
back this up.
e) Describing traumatic beatings which would have left
more sign of blood in the soil of reputed crime scene
than tests...

[Report ends here. Next page is missing.]

HE WAS WAITING IN FRONT OF THE SCHOOL TO PICK UP JAMYANG.
The bell would ring, and he would collect the child, and he would take
him to his mother. An older boy, a boy too old for this school, was
locking his bike at the fence. His shoes were purple and black.

You waiting for your son? the boy asked Wade.

He'd seen Wade here before.

He's not mine, said Wade.

He said, I'm just a friend.

Children were playing in the yard. The boy was waiting for his
little cousin, who was in Jamyang's class. It was clear to Wade that
these children were imprisoned. A dark cloud of mommies and daddies
and contests and games was visibly crushing them into shapes. The
boy was fondling his cellphone. Everyone had these appendages now,
and he couldn't remember why that woman had been so concerned.
Children were easier to keep track of, but they'd probably become better at outsmarting their parents.

I am not a monster, thought Wade.

The boy's little cousin came to the fence and smiled at them. Wade
liked the boy with the bike and he liked the little cousin, who was
self-contained and flirtatious.

Pick me up, the little boy said.

He pushed his lips through the chain-link fence.

You're over there, said Wade. And I'm over here.

You could come over here with me, suggested the boy.

Wade furrowed his brow in an exaggerated way, as if he was thinking it over.

I wish that bell would ring, said the little boy's cousin.

If Wade picked up this boy and kissed him, he thought, he wouldn't
be a monster, although he'd surely be arrested. If he were to pick up
this boy and feel his ass, that wouldn't make him a monster either. If he
were to carry the boy into the woods on the other side of the yard and
rape him, he still wouldn't be a monster. Murder the child and sexually
mutilate the corpse? Still: just a man.

Why would anyone kill a boy? So they wouldn't tell on you, he
guessed. And so nobody else could have the little prize, who'd remain
pure, private, and dead. This was a cliché, but child murderers' minds

probably operated that way, in clichés. Wanting to create a certain poignancy: a flower destroyed in earliest bloom, etc.

Murder was a bore, most likely. The point was to become a different kind of human altogether. Wade thought that he could never be a monster. He'd rather be a doorway out. It wasn't him, it was them. By "them" he meant the school, parents, and the like. He didn't mean that trite business that everyone's a monster inside. It wasn't exactly that being Hitler or Florence Nightingale was the same sort of thing. Was it that institutions were all monstrous and individuals slightly less so? He didn't know what he meant really. He hoped he'd never be reincarnated and have to grow up as a person all over again.

There wasn't much a parent wouldn't do. Wade once met a man whose mother had named him Jezebel. He went by George, but his birth certificate told another story. Other people had believed in crib death, but then they caught the mothers on video, smothering their babies with pillows.

You ever been in those woods? he asked the boy with the bike.

Why? said the boy. What's in the woods?

Is it wolves in there? asked his little cousin.

Wade gazed at the shimmering darkness over there, on the other side of the yard. It was green, and shadows, and green.

It's just trees, he said.

Jamyang's teacher emerged from the classroom with the children neatly arranged in symmetrical rows. Jamyang saw Wade, and waved.

Why aren't you with your class? the boy with the bike asked his cousin. His cousin shrugged.

It's the bell, he said. I think the bell is fittin to ring.

WADE RETURNED TO THAT CITY, THE SCENE OF THE CRIME, AND wandered around hillsides for days that turned into a week, never finding a familiar landscape or a house with a circular drive and a porch door on the cityside. Up and down the crackly hillsides, under the blazing sun.

One day a cop car ascended slowly the road he was climbing, disappeared briefly around bends and then reappeared nearer and higher until it pulled up alongside him. The men inside had no kind of face.

You headed somewhere in particular? he was asked.

I'm looking for some people, Wade said. I went to their house at night, but it all looks different in the daylight.

He smiled at them in a harmless sort of way.

You've been around for a little while now, said the driving cop. Must be real anxious to find these people. Friends?

Wade nodded.

It was on the top of one of these hills, he said. You could see out over the whole city.

The cop shook his head.

That's impossible, he said. No houses on the tops. It's against the zoning.

Wade looked puzzled.

Maybe you have us confused with some other city, suggested the other cop.

I'd suggest that you move on along, said the first. Maybe you'll find your supposed friends and their supposed house in another city.

They just sat there and looked at him.

That would mean turning around and walking down the hill, the first cop instructed him.

Have I committed some crime? asked Wade. What's the issue here?

Hasn't been a crime *yet*, said the first cop. Far as we *know*. We're just trying to keep that state of affairs in place. In fact, that's our job. We do have ordinances involving vagrancy, loitering with intent, that could be broadly interpreted. If that was our want.

He smiled at Wade. Wade nodded and descended toward the city. The cops continued up, and around a bend out of sight. Later, as he was nearing the bottom, they passed him coming down. The cops didn't look at him, and he kept right on walking.

THE DOWNTOWN WAS QUAINT. IT WAS SEASIDE AND HALF-ASSED. Just off it was a comic book store. That fact alone made Wade dizzy.

He recognized the cover immediately, among a few others of large-breasted women making eyes at masked men, large-breasted women on horseback, in the "underground" corner. This corner had a big round mirror overhead, and was directly in view of the longhaired guy at the cash register. The clerk had something kinky about him. His top half was a little too narrow, which called attention to his tight pants and his crotch. Wade placed the one he wanted in a position easy to grab. Kids were the clerk's main concern, on the other side of the store. Their bikes leaned against the window. The phone rang and the clerk turned to the side. Although he had money, Wade shoved the comic under his shirt, then stood with his hands in his pockets. Slowly browsed his way to the door.

THE BEACH HAD THE QUALITY OF AN UNWANTED PET. DOMES-ticated, yet not cared for. As he looked for a place to sit, the cop car pulled into the lot and slowly circled. He waved. They smiled and kept going.

The ocean again. He remembered that he'd thought it was beautiful and boring. Insects were biting him. Then again, he could get up and leave whenever he wanted.

He sat in the sand and read.

The comic was disappointing. Each panel, whether square or rect-angular, proceeded quite logically into the next. The plot was clear; there was nothing missing, and the characters only got what they deserved. The villains were punished, and all of the clues were ex-plained. The detectives were distinct. There was no confusion between some criminals and their victims; in fact, there was nothing there to lead a person to believe some horrible crime had taken place at all.

STEPHEN BEACHY is the author of three novels, *boneyard*, *The Whistling Song* and *Distortion*. His fiction has appeared in *Best Gay American Fiction*, *BOMB*, *The Chicago Review*, *Blithe House Quarterly*, and elsewhere, and his nonfiction and critical essays have appeared in such places as *New York Magazine*, *The New York Times Magazine*, and the *San Francisco Bay Guardian*. Raised by Mennonites "somewhere in the Midwest," he now lives in California, where he teaches at the University of San Francisco.